Hearts *racing.*
Blood *pumping.*
Pulses *accelerating.*

Falling in love can be a blur...
especially at 180 mph!

So if you crave the thrill of the chase—on and off the track—you'll love

DANGER ZONE by Debra Webb!

One million dollars.
Or her daughter would die.

Grief wrenched a cry from her throat. The anguished sound ricocheted in the deserted silence around her.

She could not let this man hurt her baby!

How could this have happened? The realization hit with shattering impact. *He knew.*

But that couldn't be. No one knew. She hadn't told a single soul the father's name.

And yet this man knew.

Jenna staggered to her feet and walked mindlessly toward her car.

Calling *him* was out of the question. She couldn't just call. After all these years, telling a man that he had a twelve-year-old daughter and then asking for a million dollars was something that had to be done in person.

She would go to him.

What would she do if he said no? Dear God, what would she do?

Dear Reader,

Growing up in Alabama, I was aware that there were two certain things about life—football and racing. The roar of the engines as those cars careered around the track generated some major excitement that I still remember vividly. It wasn't until I decided to write two NASCAR stories for Harlequin Books that I realized just what a monumental undertaking being a part of a NASCAR team really was. The undying loyalty and the incredible commitment required to be successful is mind-boggling. NASCAR drivers are not just cute guys in slick suits—they are extensively trained, fiercely focused athletes who give their all to the sport and to the fans. So next time you're watching that sexy driver thread his lean body into the car, remember that he has spent years developing the skill required to make the race you're about to see breath-stealing, edge-of-your-seat entertainment!

Even though the Rocket City Racers are fictional, if Huntsville, Alabama, had a team I am certain that is what it would be called. So turn the page and dive into life beyond the track. Follow Buck and Jenna and the rest of the Rocket City Racers on this frightening journey through a parent's worst nightmare.

Best,

Debra Webb

NASCAR

DANGER ZONE

Debra Webb

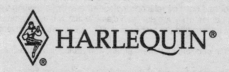

HARLEQUIN®

TORONTO • NEW YORK • LONDON
AMSTERDAM • PARIS • SYDNEY • HAMBURG
STOCKHOLM • ATHENS • TOKYO • MILAN • MADRID
PRAGUE • WARSAW • BUDAPEST • AUCKLAND

ISBN-13: 978-0-373-21770-0
ISBN-10:   0-373-21770-6

DANGER ZONE

Copyright © 2007 by Harlequin Books S.A.

Debra Webb is acknowledged as the author of this work.

NASCAR® and the NASCAR Library Collection are registered trademarks of the National Association for Stock Car Auto Racing, Inc.

This edition published by arrangement with Harlequin Books S.A.

® and TM are trademarks of the publisher. Trademarks indicated with ® are registered in the United States Patent and Trademark Office, the Canadian Trade Marks Office and in other countries.

www.eHarlequin.com

Printed in U.S.A.

DEBRA WEBB

Debra Webb's romantic-suspense publishing career was launched in September 2000. Since then this award-winning, bestselling author has had more than fifty novels published. Visit her on the Web at www.debrawebb.com or write to her at P.O. Box 64, Huntland, TN 37345.

Danger Zone is dedicated to all the devoted racing fans who are the very heart and soul of the sport.

CHAPTER ONE

Jackson County Hospital
Scottsboro, Alabama

THE LOUNGE DOOR flew open, Dr. Carla Blake stuck her head in and shouted, "Brace yourselves people, we've got victims from a five-car pileup coming through the doors any minute! We're going to need all hands."

Jenna Williams sighed and closed her locker, leaving her purse and coat inside. It happened every time she agreed to work an extra half shift. No matter that she'd been there since two that morning and it was now four in the afternoon, fate would see that going home wasn't an option for at least another hour. That it was Friday only stacked the odds against her. But that was the life of an E.R. nurse. Sometimes it was plain old inconvenient, but she loved her work and it paid the bills.

Two other nurses, along with one intern, who'd worked the extra-long shift exchanged weary glances with her, but not one complained out loud. Instead the group shuffled back out to the E.R. floor. Arguing or complaining would be pointless. When Dr. Blake spoke, the E.R. listened. She hadn't been dubbed *the dictator* for nothing.

Once the ambulances rolled in, thoughts of going home or the unfairness of it all vanished. The world narrowed until nothing else existed.

Gurneys rushed through the emergency entrance with paramedics shouting information about their patients.

Jenna jumped into the organized chaos, her movements instinctive and in precisely timed rhythm with her coworkers. Twelve victims arrived, two critical.

Just over ninety minutes later both criticals were in surgery and holding their own. Six of the other patients had been treated and released and the remaining four were admitted for observation related to moderate head injuries. The E.R. was quiet again and the exhausted staff released a collective sigh of relief. Not losing a patient after a major pileup was something to celebrate.

"Got any plans this weekend?"

Jenna glanced up from her locker and gave her friend Gina Daniels a *you're kidding* look. "Ballet practice with Bec. We're gearing up for recital. We'll be practicing every Saturday morning and Sunday afternoon from now until the end of May."

Gina sidled up next to her as if what she had to say was top secret. "Dale asked me out."

Jenna's lips spread into a genuine smile despite the clawing fatigue. "Really? When did this happen?" Dale and Gina had been dancing around the concept of dating for weeks now.

"Lunch." Gina looked around covertly. "He fell into line behind me and popped the question between the salad bar and the cash register."

Shouldering into her coat, Jenna pressed for more details. It wasn't every day that a single nurse snagged the hottest new resident. At least not in this small town, where new residents were as scarce as a lunar eclipse. "Where's he taking you?" Her own social life was so dead that she'd long ago decided that living vicariously through her friend was about the only excitement she could hope for.

"The Jazz Factory in Huntsville." She grinned. "And after dinner, we're going dancing."

Jenna's eyes rounded. "Dr. Dale dances?"

Dr. Dale Parker was not only one of the hottest new residents at Jackson County Hospital, he was brilliant. Everyone loved him. And he was nice, really nice. Every unattached female at the hospital had her sights set on him.

"Evidently he does," Gina confirmed. She winked. "I hope he can horizontal mambo."

"You are bad," Jenna teased, a flush heating her face. It had been so long since she'd had sex that just the idea of it flustered her. It was tough to have sex when she wasn't even dating. It was equally tough because she was a mother whose twelve-year-old daughter required a full-time chauffeur and endless attention.

"If I'm lucky," Gina hissed under her breath, "I'll be *real* bad."

Jenna grabbed her purse and closed her locker for what she hoped would be the last time until Monday. She didn't often get both Saturday and Sunday off, and she was definitely looking forward to spending lots of time with her daughter. A beleaguered sigh slipped past her lips. No date. No sex. Oh well, being a good mother and a dedicated nurse would just have to be enough.

"Oh, damn." Jenna glanced at her watch. It was 5:40 p.m. "Bec had soccer practice today."

"On Friday?" Gina opened the door to the lounge and waited for Jenna to go ahead of her.

"This is the first time most of the kids on the team have played soccer," she explained as they moved into the corridor that would take them to an exit-only side door, avoiding any possibility of running into the dictator. "The coach thinks they need a little extra practice for a few weeks."

Jenna was glad to see Bec participating in a school sport. She'd been dancing since she was big enough to walk. Ballet, tap, jazz. Dance had consumed her life. Her daughter had high hopes of going to Juilliard after high school. And though that was a ways off for a seventh grader, she never lost her focus. Even with the soccer her daughter insisted would build stamina and make her a better dancer, the unavoidable bruises not withstanding.

Jenna had a feeling that her daughter's sudden obsession with soccer had more to do with a particular young man who played on the boy's team than with building stamina. It was hard to believe her little girl was growing up so fast. In a few months she'd be an actual teenager…thirteen. Where had the time gone?

The temperature outside had dropped considerably after sunset. The wind whipped at her face, nipping her ears and slapping her cheeks with its bitter sting. Jenna pulled her black wool coat more tightly around her and wished she hadn't forgotten her scarf. The weather in northern Alabama at the end of January and beginning of February was the absolute worst.

With a promise to call with all the juicy date details, Jenna and Gina parted ways in the parking lot. Jenna climbed into her ancient Volkswagen Bug, a '72 orange original with all the miles and constant need for new parts that came with the label *vintage*.

Jenna removed the clip that kept her hair tucked neatly into a makeshift bun and shook her head. It felt good to let her hair down after a twelve-hour shift that had lasted fifteen and a half. Then she took a deep breath and pushed all thoughts of work away. Time to relax and enjoy the weekend with her girl.

Scottsboro Junior High was in the middle of town,

just off the courthouse square. Bec always waited at the little stone bridge next to the bus stop. But this time her daughter wasn't there. The schoolyard was deserted.

Okay, maybe practice had gone overtime. Jenna drove around to the back of the school where the practice field was actually the expansive backyard of a home on College Street. But the field was deserted, as well. That didn't really surprise her since practice had ended, according to the coach's schedule, more than half an hour ago.

She parked along the curb and got out. Pulling her collar up around her ears, she headed for the coach's office. He usually hung around for a while after the kids were gone. But not today. The entrance to the athletic office was locked. The corridor beyond was dark as far as she could see through the small window in the door.

"Well, darn."

Maybe one of her friends had given Becca a ride home? The guilt started its downward press on her shoulders. She'd done this twice already and the season had scarcely started. Good mothers didn't leave their kids in the lurch like this. Jenna's mother usually picked Bec up after school, except on practice days. If Jenna had only had time to call her mother before the chaos had hit the E.R. she could have avoided this worrisome moment altogether.

No way to change that now. After fishing her phone from her purse she called home. Five rings, no answer. The machine picked up. "Bec, if you're there give me a call and let me know you're home."

Next Jenna called her mother. "Mom, did Becca come to your house after practice?"

The "no" that echoed across the line sent a prick of alarm through Jenna but she banished it. There were still several more places she could be.

"I'm sure everything's fine," she told her mom. "I'll check with Coach Bob."

Her fingers stumbled as she quickly entered the number for Coach Robert Riley. Jenna felt some relief at just hearing his voice when he answered. "Hey, Coach, this is Jenna Williams, Becca's mom." She waited as he launched into how much her daughter had improved and how hard she worked. Jenna's heart had started to thud even as she told herself again that everything was fine. As soon as he paused for a breath, she asked, "Listen, did someone give Bec a ride home? I'm here at the school and she's not around."

She held her breath as she waited for him to consider the question. Her heart slowed instantly upon hearing his answer. Her daughter had left with one of her friends. Thank goodness. Coach Bob had seen her get in the car. He just didn't recall which friend. "Thanks, Coach. Sorry I was late today. Big accident over on the interstate. I'll check with Bec's friends."

Relief making her knees a little unsteady, Jenna

started at the top of the list—Bec's best friend, Carrie Melberger.

"Hey, Carrie, did Becca ride home with you?"

The "no, ma'am" that resounded in Jenna's ear launched the new, heavy thud in her chest.

"Okay, thanks."

Jenna stood in the middle of that deserted parking lot. She forgot about the cold, as she made seven or eight more calls. She lost exact count as desperation and sheer terror took hold.

"You're sure you didn't see who was driving the car?" she asked the coach, who had called her back. He'd wanted to make sure Jenna had found Bec. As he described the car, a beep signaled that Jenna had another call. She held the cell away from her ear long enough to identify the number on the display.

Bec's cell number flashed on the display.

Thank God!

Jenna rested the phone against her ear once more. "I'm getting a call from her cell now, Coach." The burst of relief left her weak and shaky. "Thanks for your help." She hit the necessary buttons and almost shouted, "Young lady, do you know how frantic I've been? Where are you?"

The long beat of silence that passed caused the bottom to drop out of Jenna's stomach.

"Bec?"

"Have no fear, Ms. Williams, your daughter is safe here with me."

The voice sounded male but it was garbled or distorted so that she couldn't say for sure.

"Who is this?" The question came from her but her own voice sounded foreign to her ears. Hollow and small. Not the voice of a hardcore E.R. nurse accustomed to barking statistics and necessary responses.

"Ms. Williams, we have important business to discuss."

Ice slid through her veins. "I'm...sorry." She licked her trembling lips. "I don't understand." *Please, God, don't let this be happening.*

"If you want to see your little girl alive again you must do exactly as I say."

Jenna held on to the phone with both hands, fear making her fingers so numb she was certain she might drop it at any second. "Please, don't hurt her." *Please, please, please.*

"I won't hurt her," the cruel, garbled voice assured. "As long as you do as I say. Make one mistake and the next time you see your daughter will be at the morgue for identification purposes."

"I'll do anything you ask." Fear and tears crowded into Jenna's throat, making it nearly impossible to breathe. "Anything."

"I hope you mean what you say, Ms. Williams, otherwise your daughter will be a very dead little girl."

"Just tell me what to do. Please," she begged. Questions whirled in her head. What was happening?

Who was this man? Why would he take her child? Was this someone she knew? Someone she'd met at the hospital…a mental patient she'd dealt with? She didn't know…she just didn't know.

"I will call you again in exactly twenty-four hours," he said, snapping her to attention. "At that time I will give you instructions for the exchange."

Exchange?

She moistened her lips and reached way down deep for her courage. "What kind of exchange?" She thought of the piddling savings she had in the bank for Bec's college plans. It wasn't much but maybe it would be enough.

"I will give your daughter back to you, in the same condition I found her, in exchange for one million dollars. Cash."

A million dollars?

Her heart dropped all the way to the cold asphalt beneath her feet. "How…" She cleared her throat. "I don't have that kind of money. I might—"

"Not a penny less, Ms. Williams. One million dollars, *exactly.*"

Dear God, what would she do?

"Please…" What did she say? How did she make him understand without the risk of making him angry? "I'm just a nurse. I don't have any way to raise that kind of money."

"Surely you know someone with access to large sums of cash."

Her head was shaking jerkily but he couldn't see. "No. I'm sorry. I don't know anyone that rich." The names of her friends, her relatives, all rushed through her head. No one with resources like that.

"If you contact the police your daughter will die."

Her legs gave way. Jenna dropped to her knees on the cold, hard pavement. "Please, you don't understand—"

"I will be watching your every move," he cut in sharply, "and monitoring your calls. Do you understand this, Ms. Williams?"

"Yes. Yes."

"At six-fifteen tomorrow evening I will call. Have the money and be prepared to make the exchange."

"But if I can't get that much…" She couldn't say the rest. Her body shook so violently she could hardly think.

"There must be someone you can turn to, Ms. Williams," the twisted voice urged. "Think. I'm sure there's someone you're overlooking."

And then she knew.

There was someone.

"Twenty-four hours, Ms. Williams. I will call. You will have the million dollars or she dies."

He severed the connection.

Jenna stared at the phone in her hand for seconds that turned into a full minute before she had the presence of mind to close it.

One million dollars.

Or her daughter would die.

Grief wrenched from her throat. The anguished cry ricocheted in the deserted silence around her.

She could not let this man hurt her baby!

How could this have happened? The realization hit with shattering impact.

He knew.

But that couldn't be. How could he possibly know? No one knew. She hadn't told a single soul the father's name.

And yet, this man knew.

Jenna staggered to her feet and walked mindlessly toward her car.

Calling *him* was out of the question. She couldn't just call.

After all these years, telling a man that he had a twelve-year-old daughter and then asking for a million dollars was something that had to be done in person.

She would go to him.

Jenna collapsed into the driver's seat. She'd need pictures so he could see that she was telling the truth.

And then she would beg for the money.

She didn't care what she had to do to convince him. As long as she got the money within twenty-four hours. She wanted to be ready and waiting when the kidnapper called back.

She reached for the key in the ignition. She hadn't seen *him* in over thirteen years. But he had always been a reasonable man when it came to the facts. She had never known him to turn away anyone in need. His generosity was part of who he was. He surely wouldn't have changed that much.

Her fingers twisted the key, starting the engine.

But what if he refused? Her chest tightened with a new kind of fear. He might not even want to see her. Thirteen years was a long time.

Another bitter reality closed in on her. What would she do if he said no?

Dear God, what would she do?

Whatever it took.

CHAPTER TWO

Buchanan Building
Huntsville, Alabama

GO FOR THE GOLD.

The slogan Buck Buchanan was using to launch the Rocket City Racers into this year's racing season was a smash hit. He saw it everywhere. The fans loved it and, evidently, so did the media. The fact that NASCAR drivers were being recognized as true athletes, just as those going for the gold in the Olympics, was being heralded in most every article related to the coming season.

Buck's team was ready.

He was ready.

Giving the remote a click to turn off the plasma television as the news brief came to a close, he rose from his chair. 7:00 p.m. Time to go home.

For some reason the idea of going to his empty house alone felt particularly unappealing tonight. He'd been doing it for years, no need for things to be any different this evening. Yet, somehow it was.

A tap at his office door preceded its opening. Having Rush Jackson, his driver, step into his office surprised him. He'd thought everyone else had gone home already. With Daytona just around the corner they all needed to pack and get ready to leave in a few days.

"Rush, what're you doing hanging around here at this hour? Max will have your hide." Buck felt confident Rush's new bride, Maxine Gray, wouldn't appreciate sitting at home alone on Friday night.

"There's something you need to see, Buck," Rush urged. He hitched his thumb toward the door. "I think we have a leak of some sort going on in the den."

Uneasiness trickled through Buck. A leak in the structure of this building he could handle. Any other kind…he didn't even want to think about. The sting of betrayal by one of his closest confidants was still way too strong to have to go down that road again so soon.

"What kind of leak?"

Rush's brow furrowed in perplexity. "Well…it's kind of hard to explain…." He cleared his throat. "You'll just have to come see for yourself."

Buck rounded his desk and followed Rush down the hall to the den, which had actually been a massive conference room when Buck first bought the building. He'd turned it into a cozy den where he and his team hashed out the business of racing. There was something cold and unfeeling about conference rooms. This way, they worked out their problems like kin.

Rush flipped on the light as they entered the room.

"Surprise!"

The first thing to snag Buck's attention was the streamers.

Crimson and white.

And lots of black balloons floating around like ominous clouds threatening rain.

"What the hell?"

The room full of people broke into a chorus of "Happy Birthday."

Buck didn't fight the fact that there was probably a pretty goofy smile on his face. Mostly one of surprise. But he couldn't quite seem to shift his lips into any other position. Goofy would just have to do.

Today was his birthday. Forty years old.

He'd tried not to think about it, not because he cared that he'd reached a new bracket on a life insurance form, but because he had been feeling a little off the past few days. Not exactly old…but something along those lines.

The applause and the cheering that followed the song had him bowing graciously. He loved these folks. Along with his sister, they were his family. All he really needed.

A hollow ache attempted to contradict that last thought. He didn't need anyone or anything else, he reiterated mentally. Whatever the heck was making him feel out-of-whack lately would just have to find somebody else's head to mess with. Buck Buchanan liked his life exactly the way it was. Focused.

The cake was huge. White cake, with white icing—his favorite. *The big 4-0* was emblazoned in crimson across the white top—crimson and white being the team's colors.

"Make a wish and blow out the candles!" Lori Houser, the team's public relations expert, shouted.

"If you can muster up the strength," George Farley, his crew chief, ribbed.

There were a hell of a lot of candles flickering away in front of him. But he'd never backed away from an honest challenge.

"Make a wish first," Reba, his sister, reminded. "But don't say it out loud if you want it to come true."

A wish. She'd always believed in wishes, even when they were kids and didn't have a damned thing to wish for. But everything was different for them now. He'd seen to that.

What in the world did a man like him, who had it all, wish for?

A vision of long, silky black hair and blue-gray eyes flashed in his mind. God Almighty, how could he still think of *her* that way? Truth be told he'd thought of her many times, usually in his dreams. They would make love like they used to and things would end very differently from the way they had in real life.

But those were dreams. This was real life.

Buck gulped in a big breath and blew with all his might until the flames dancing atop every single candle had been extinguished.

Another round of cheers and applause followed.

His good friends, people he trusted, including members of the local television news channels as well as the *Huntsville Times,* had come to celebrate. All wanted to shake his hand and offer their best wishes. Every single member of his team and their significant others were present. As were Reba, his only blood kin, and her husband, Lowell.

He was a hell of a lucky guy.

"A toast!" Rush Jackson announced as he popped the cork on a bottle of bubbly. Another cork or two were wrenched from other bottles and glasses were filled to overflowing. Rush poured one for Buck then one for himself. He held the glass high. "To the best team owner in NASCAR!"

The toast resounded in the gathered crowd. Buck nodded his appreciation and drank deeply from his glass. The champagne fizzed down his throat.

This was what his life was really all about. His friends. The racing. Hell, he'd been told the better part of his adult life that racing fuel ran through his veins. And maybe it did. A man should feel good about his accomplishments. No regrets.

Kicking aside the negative feelings, Buck mingled, took the time that wasn't always available during the heat of the season just to chat with good friends.

He'd had his second glass of champagne and was feeling warm and pleasant when Scott Jameson from the *Times* had to bring up the dead-last thing Buck ever wanted to talk about again.

Tom McElroy.

"I heard he moved out to Austin. Bought himself a ranch there."

Buck couldn't very well get fired up at Jameson for bringing up the issue. No one knew the real story. Only Buck's team and a select few within NASCAR. Keeping McElroy's dirty deeds under wraps had been the right thing to do. For the team and the sport. Making a public spectacle of the whole debacle would have served no purpose whatsoever. It would serve none now.

"Yeah," Buck confirmed what Jameson had heard. "He'd always talked about retiring to Texas one day."

"Does this mean you're thinking of retiring in the near future?" Jameson nudged, ever the newsman.

Buck laughed and decided that laughing was a far better response than telling him where he could stick the idea of retirement. "No way. I couldn't live without the roar of those engines."

That was the God's truth. Buck was certain he wouldn't survive a single day without his team to manage…without the thrill of hearing those engines start. He was an adrenaline junkie through and through. He didn't deny it.

"Time to open your present, Buck." Charlene

Talley, their top spotter, grabbed his arm and dragged him to the table on the far side of the room.

A big box wrapped in shiny black paper with a sheer black ribbon tied around it waited. Black roses had been left across its top as if it were a coffin rather than a gift box.

"Very nice," he said, cutting a look at a couple of his team members, both of whom he felt certain were instrumental behind this shenanigan.

"Just open it," David Mason, the chief mechanic, urged.

Buck set the black roses aside, then ripped open the ribbon and paper. He lifted the top off the carton and the sides fell away. A collective gasp reverberated in the room.

An exact replica of No. 86—his car…the team's car—sat atop a mahogany-and-brass base. As he examined it he realized this wasn't just any sort of model, this was a precision-crafted, exact replica with every imaginable working part. Written across the brass plaque on the base was the team's motto: *Eighty-six the competition!* The piece had to have cost a small fortune, not to mention the work to build. It had likely taken months if not a year.

He turned to the members of his team and grappled for the right words, fought with his emotions to keep his voice steady. "Is this the best you could do?"

Laughter lightened the moment, but as he hugged

one hardworking member of his team after the other, he felt the connection. The bond that made the Rocket City Racers special.

His sister, Reba, left early because she was heading out to a sales conference at the crack of dawn the next morning. By the time the last of the crowd had gone home, it was past nine o'clock. Rush and Max had helped Buck select a place on the credenza beneath the plasma TV for the model, since that was the most prominent spot in the den. He wanted everyone to be able to enjoy the beautiful piece of artwork. And it was definitely art. Just like the real No. 86 flying around the track was pure art in motion.

Buck pulled on his coat, turned out the lights and took the stairs down to the lobby. The Buchanan Building sat in the heart of Huntsville, the city he loved.

Outside he hunched his shoulders to usher the collar of his coat up around his ears. It was cold out here. The sky was clear so not much chance of any precipitation. He climbed into his black Escalade and headed toward home. He'd built a big house in the Hampton Cove community more than a dozen years ago at his sister's urging. As a real estate agent she had insisted that he needed to get more property investments in his portfolio.

The drive over the mountain from Huntsville proper to the Cove was dark and quiet, almost somber…like his mood. There was no cause for it, he reminded himself.

What more could a man ask for?

There was just no reason for this wholly uncharacteristic feeling of emptiness.

Buck turned down the drive that wound through the trees and landscape of his property. Suddenly he realized that he'd just hit forty and had never been married, certainly had no prospects.

Funny, his single status hadn't really bothered him before. He wasn't about to let a midlife crisis sneak up on him now as a few of his acquaintances had done.

He didn't bother parking in the garage, just got out and went inside. Good thing the alarm signaled that he needed to enter his code or he would have forgotten it. He was that distracted with the ridiculous notion that coming home alone, as he did most of the time, was somehow wrong tonight.

He'd had a great birthday. His whole world was just as it should be. He had no right to be feeling sorry for himself for still being single.

"Stupid, Buchanan." He tossed his keys onto the table. The plop echoed in the empty entryhall and he flinched.

Truth was, he was alone.

Yeah, he had his team and his sister. He had money, prestige, most everything a man of his age would want. So he couldn't actually claim loneliness. But he was now forty and he didn't have a woman in his life. He thought of his sister and her husband...of Rush and his new bride. Not having a significant other at forty…well, that meant alone. No way to deny it. However, that didn't mean he was going to mope around here feeling sorry for himself.

Hell, no.

He dated from time to time. But between the team and the need to stay on top in this business, he was too busy to spend much time on his social life. Lots of men his age were still single. It wasn't as if he'd avoided marriage—it just hadn't worked out and he'd never had any desire to have children. End of subject.

He turned on the lamp in the hall and made his way to the stairs. If the answer was so simple then why the heavy pressure on his chest? The overwhelming sense of weight on his shoulders?

Hesitating at the newel post, he decided that a bracing shot of bourbon was in order. Hell, it was his birthday. He was entitled to a nightcap. He pulled off his leather coat and his suit jacket, and hung both across the banister.

The great room claimed a good deal of the downstairs floor space on the left side of the entryhall. The amount of entertaining that went along with his position as team owner required a grand room for that purpose. He flipped a wall switch as he entered the room and two table lamps glowed to life. He unbuttoned his shirt and pulled it loose from his trousers as he crossed the room.

Behind the bar he selected his bourbon of choice. When he'd downed a couple of swallows, he leaned on the bar and considered all the good things in his life.

His team.

The strides he'd made in ensuring NASCAR was viewed as a true sport. The whole racing industry had come a long, long way since his heyday as a driver more than a decade ago.

He had a lot to be thankful for.

Even the recent betrayal by a close confidant and longtime friend couldn't lessen what he had attained. Not by a long shot.

And still something was missing.

Buck exhaled a weary sigh and ran his hand through his hair. It didn't take a rocket scientist to figure it out.

He didn't need just any woman.

He needed Jenna.

He could deny it all he wanted to, but it was true.

Every woman he'd ever dated had left him less than enthusiastic about seeing her a second time. How could anyone hope to measure up to a ghost from his past? No woman could. It was unfair of him to insist upon it, conscious or not.

He glanced around the elegant room an interior decorator had created. Sure his house was great, but his office felt more like home.

"Buck, you are one pitiful puppy."

He made a frustrated sound and set his unfinished drink aside. No need to go round and round about this. He knew the deal. The mood would pass when it passed. He'd almost let himself get in a similar state after Rush and Max's wedding, but he'd managed to escape that day without any lingering side effects. Maybe that event was still too fresh, combined with his turning forty—he'd evidently let the past sneak up on him.

Tom McElroy used to say that fate had its own way of mapping out a man's future. A pang of fresh hurt tore at Buck's gut. This was the first time he'd missed his former friend. Tom could always be counted on for reminding Buck of all the reasons things would never have worked out between him and *her*.

Jenna hadn't bonded with the team. She'd kept herself at arm's length when it came to his friends. They'd argued a thousand times about how he paid far more attention to the car than he did her. Every fight had ended with her certain that she played second fiddle to his one true love: racing. She just couldn't accept who he was and what he did. And he sure couldn't change. Not this side of the grave anyway.

A true tragedy. Only instead of playing out on stage, this one had played out in small-town Alabama with high speeds and all the drama expected from a rising celebrity and his entourage.

Some things, he'd had to learn the hard way, just weren't meant to be.

The doorbell chimed and he heaved a mighty breath. Tried to think who the hell would be at his door at this time of night. He glanced at the clock, almost ten.

If any of the guys had gotten cocky and decided to send him an intimate, however naughty, birthday present like they did last year, he was going to kick some serious butt. Talking that exotic dancer into going home without performing a whole routine, including a lap dance, had taken some doing, not to mention a hefty tip. Though he genuinely appreciated the thought behind the gift, that definitely wasn't his style.

Without thinking of looking through the peephole—his mind was clearly elsewhere—he deactivated the alarm, released the lock and dead bolt, then opened the front door, ready to tell whoever was there that it was the house next door they wanted. He didn't need any bought-and-paid-for company. Not tonight for sure. Tonight he wanted to dream about things that would never be. It was his birthday, he could wallow in the past if he wanted.

His gaze settled on the woman waiting outside his door and the memory of that foolish wish he'd made before blowing out his candles slammed full throttle into his gut. This wasn't supposed to happen.

Jenna.

Impossible.

He blinked, certain he was hallucinating.

"Hello, Buck."

Nope. She was real.

"Jenna?"

He kept expecting someone to jump out and shout that he'd been Punk'd, but that didn't happen.

Instead she looked at him with those blue-gray eyes he'd dreamed of a thousand times and made a statement that intrigued him and scared the living daylights out of him.

"I need your help."

CHAPTER THREE

SHE HADN'T EXPECTED this to be easy, but she was suddenly afraid asking him for the money might be harder than she had anticipated.

"Come in." Buck took her by the arm and hauled her over his threshold.

Be strong, she ordered. Becca is depending on you. The urge to cry struck again with knee-buckling force.

She restrained the shaking in her limbs.

When he'd closed and locked the door he turned back to her. "What's wrong?" He looked so startled, so worried. His shirt was open and hanging loose, his hair was rumpled. Had he been asleep?

Stop obsessing. Deep breath. Take it slow. *If you jump right in with the news you'll spook him.* All the way to Huntsville she'd told herself over and over how this should go. Take a minute to catch up, gauge his reaction to seeing her again. Get a measure on his attitude if possible. Then tell him…

After all, the last time he'd seen her she had been walking away.

Enough. Thrashing around in the past wouldn't help.

Do it the way you planned.

The order reverberated in her brain, prompting the necessary synapse.

"You look good, Buck." He did. Not older really, just more mature. She tightened her hold on the shoulder strap of her purse, giving her hands something to do.

The expression on his face told her he hadn't expected her to come across with an announcement like that.

Calm. Steady. Stay cool. Don't falter.

His mouth opened and his throat worked a moment before he found his voice. Oh, yeah, she'd stunned him, all right.

"You look good, too, Jen."

Jen. He'd always called her that. Stop. Pay attention.

"Thank you." She glanced around the entryhall. He'd been building this house when they split up. This was the first time she'd been inside. "Can we sit a few minutes?" She was reasonably sure that if she kept standing here, she'd end up a crumpled, quivering mass in the floor. She was working hard to keep her chin up and her shoulders back without locking her knees in hopes of keeping herself steady, but the need to curl up into a ball of agony was tearing at her big-time.

"God Almighty. I'm sorry," he said with a shake of his head. "Please, come on in and have a seat."

He ushered her into a room that was far too large

to be called a living room. Leather sofas and chairs. Massive entertainment center and a bar that looked like it had been taken from an English pub, polished up and planted right here in his house. Gleaming hardwood and thick, lush rugs anchored groupings of furniture.

She settled on the edge of a graceful side chair, the intricately carved wooden arms giving her something to hang on to. She dropped her purse to the floor next to her chair as he lowered his tall frame onto the sofa.

"Can I get you something to drink?"

He was analyzing her very closely now. Concern and something like amazement in his brown eyes. That he looked worried even after all these years surprised her a little. But it shouldn't have. He'd always been a kind man. She hadn't expected that to change.

"I'm…" Maybe she did need a drink. God knew she could definitely use some courage. "A drink would be good."

Her abrupt change of heart sent a flicker of uncertainty across his face. "Brandy?"

"That's fine." She wasn't a drinker, didn't even remember the last time she'd had so much as a beer.

He rose in one fluid move and walked over to the bar. "You still in Scottsboro?" he asked as he poured her drink without looking at her.

"Yes." The hurt that slashed through her at the idea that her baby was not at home or at a friend's house twisted in her belly.

He crossed back to the sofa, the glass in hand. "How's your mother?"

Jenna accepted the glass, somehow managing the feat without her hand shaking too badly. "She's fine." Before he could ask the next question she downed a gulp. The burn startled her but also reminded her of its promise.

"You might ought to sip that, darlin'."

Her gaze flew to his and a shiver of awareness rushed over her. She hated herself for it. How could she feel anything right now? Oh, God... She took another swallow.

"Jen, you said you needed my help."

She finished the last of the brandy and set the glass aside before meeting his eyes. "Yes."

He waited, that steady gaze making her come apart a little more on the inside. *Don't let it show!* she urged her crumbling composure. Be strong. For Bec.

"I need..." She moistened her lips. "I need to borrow one million dollars."

That he didn't flinch was a good sign...she hoped.

An almost imperceptible nod was accompanied by, "I see."

She tightened her grasp on the chair arms, as much to keep from throwing herself on her knees in front of him as to keep from flying into a thousand pieces of writhing agony.

"I swear I wouldn't ask if it wasn't a matter of life and death." Tears crowded into her throat.

"You're the only person I know who might be able to help me."

She knew how that sounded. The guard that had gone up in his expression told her she'd hurt him with the request. He probably had people trying to take advantage of him all the time. If there had been any other way…

"Is your mother ill?" He inclined his head, the worry taking center stage in his eyes once more. "Are you ill, Jen? A million dollars is a lot of money. What is it you're not telling me?"

Her lips trembled as she sucked in a big breath. Don't cry, she ordered. Please don't cry. "No. We're both fine." The air she'd only just managed to draw in exited in shuddering spurts. "It's…it's my… daughter."

Something like confusion, or surprise, maybe both, joined the worry on his face, but only for a fleeting second, just long enough for her to see. "I'm sure sorry to hear there's trouble. Is she in the hospital? You need the money for medical expenses?"

It would be so easy to lie. That flicker of suspicion in his eyes, the new tension in his shoulders, all of it would just fade away if she just let him believe the problem was that simple. God, she wanted to take that route. To let him believe her daughter was sick and in need of some major surgery or organ transplant that would require such a huge sum of money. She could take the money and go home to wait for that call.

But she knew that would be wrong. She felt it in every fiber of her being. How could she beg God to help her, then sit here and lie outright to this man?

She said one final prayer for strength, then she did what she knew in her heart was right. "I went to the school to pick her up after soccer practice today." Her throat constricted, holding her mute a second, and then another.

"Soccer? Is she any good?" he asked, clearly attempting to set her at ease.

Jen nodded jerkily. *Calm,* she reminded herself. Don't panic. He hadn't said no...yet. "The coach says she's really improving. This is her first year. She usually dances." Her chest tightened with the need to tell this man what a beautiful dancer his daughter was. How graceful...how truly talented. She reined in the urge. Reminded herself to go slowly. Be concise, rational.

"Something happened at soccer practice?" he prompted.

The image of that empty soccer field forced its way into her thoughts. The terror renewed with ice-cold intensity, making her shudder. "She wasn't there."

Something in the eyes assessing her so closely changed, altered significantly with her answer. Gone was the suspicion, replaced by a natural protective instinct she had seen before.

She had to look away. "I called my mom, the coach, all her friends, but she wasn't with any of them." She stared at the white knuckles of her hands where she clutched the chair arms. "I was terrified."

His big hand covered her right one, the one closest to him. "I can imagine. You called the police?"

Her gaze collided with his at the mention of the police. Buck would insist she call them. She couldn't. The kidnapper said not to. Ignoring his question, she said, "I got a call." The fear rose, expanded so rapidly in her chest she was sure she'd have a heart attack. There was no holding back the tears, they brimmed, then poured down her cheeks. But she no longer cared. "If I don't give the man who took my daughter a million dollars he's going to—" her throat constricted again "—kill my baby."

His fingers tightened around her hand, pulled her out of her chair. He scooted over and ushered her down onto the sofa next to him. "Take it slow, darlin', and tell me exactly what he said."

She couldn't stop the shaking now. Buck's strong arm around her was probably all that kept her upright. She repeated what the garbled voice had said as close to word-for-word as her worried mind could manage.

"You didn't call the police?" he asked again.

She shook her head adamantly. "He told me what would happen if I did. I can't take the risk." That one drink had started to warm her, as the quaking had eased somewhat.

The seconds lapsed into a minute with Buck con-

sidering all that she had told him. Was he debating
the believability of her story? What if he turned her
down? She should tell him the rest. She opened her
mouth to do so but then he spoke again.

"I'll do whatever I can to help you, Jen, there's no
question." That steady, penetrating gaze backed up
his words. "You don't need to worry about that."

Thank God. She swiped at her eyes and tried to
smile, but her quivering lips just couldn't make the
transition. "Thank you."

"But I need to ask you a few questions."

A new tension made her rigid. Was he looking for
a graceful way to bow out of this? Maybe he didn't
really want to give her the money. It was an awful lot.
They hadn't seen each other in years. She had to be
crazy to think he would simply give her the money
and let it go at that.

"Don't worry," he assured as if he'd heard her
thoughts. "You have my word that I'll help you. You
said he wouldn't call again until tomorrow evening,
so there's time. Okay?"

She nodded. Buck wouldn't back out on her. She
knew him better than that. Once Buck Buchanan
committed, he was in for the long haul, good, bad or
indifferent. He was kind and generous and selflessly
giving of himself…to a point. But there was a line
he had drawn when it came to giving away his heart.
She'd stood squarely on the other side of the line for
far too long.

Stop. This was about now. About Becca. The past was over and done with.

"You have no idea who would do this?"

"No." She didn't even have to think about it. No one she knew would want to hurt Bec and certainly no one in her life would even consider asking her for that kind of money. She was just a nurse who did a little better than simply getting by, but not much.

"This part might be none of my business, but I have to ask."

She peered up at him expectantly. How could she deny him anything he wanted to ask? He was going to help her. That was all that mattered.

"What about her father? Would he be capable of doing anything like this? If he knew of our connection, he might have hatched up this plan to cash in on it, so to speak."

How on earth did she answer that question? Did she tell him the truth? She'd come prepared to do that…but now she was so afraid. "He…he wouldn't do that."

"You're certain?" Buck pressed.

"Yes." Somehow she managed to look him in the eye. "Bec's father is out of the picture."

That made him sound like a creep. It wasn't fair. Buck didn't even know he had a daughter. She'd wanted to tell him all those years ago. But she'd known better. Buck Buchanan had not wanted children. He'd been adamant about it. He'd told her that a child wouldn't have fit into his world, but she knew it went far deeper than that. Buck had issues where kids were concerned. He loved kids as long as they belonged to someone else. She wasn't oblivious to the news about all the donations he made to the children's hospital and numerous shelters for abused women and children.

But she knew the real story behind his need to reach out that way and yet refuse to have children of his own. His own abusive father had walked out on him when he was nine. Raising two kids all alone had taken a toll on his mother, and had caused tremendous hardship for their small family.

Whether he would ever admit it or not, Jenna was certain his father's betrayal was why Buck had decided long ago that he would not do the dad thing. She'd always wondered if maybe he didn't trust himself. Fear that he would fail somehow had kept him clear of that line he'd drawn as a frightened child.

When she'd discovered she was pregnant, despite their precautions, she had known telling him would be a mistake. Their relationship had been on shaky ground as it was, and adding into the mix a child he surely didn't want would not have made things right.

Telling him now might not be the right thing to do, either. She didn't have the time or the energy to debate the question or to deal with the argument that would no doubt follow the announcement. Her first and only concern had to be about getting her daughter back.

"If you're certain about that," he said in response to her assertion that Bec's father wasn't a part of their lives, "we'll operate under the assumption that this is someone you don't know. Someone who knows you'd come to me for the money, and who possibly has some idea that we were once a couple."

A couple. No, never a couple. The relationship had never been that simple. There was always her and Buck, of course, but there was also the team, the track, the fans, the racing. Buck was not an entity unto himself. He was a part of a package. But she said none of that. It didn't matter now.

"That's the only answer I could come up with," she agreed. "He almost prompted me to that conclusion. He said something like was I sure I didn't know someone…that there must be someone I was overlooking who could help me." She shuddered at the memory of that cruel, garbled voice.

Buck's arm tightened protectively around her shoulders. "I'm sorry this happened, Jen. But I promise you I'll do all within my power to help get your daughter back."

She couldn't look at him. He might see the lie in her eyes. Telling him the rest would only complicate things. She was right about that, wasn't she? "Thank you."

Guilt crushed in on her even as she assured herself she'd made the right choice. How could she sit here like this? Take his comfort and ask for his money and not tell him the truth?

What did that make her?

But the truth would only open up a whole other set of problems, she argued. There would be questions. Anger. Bitterness. She didn't need any of that right now. The focus had to be on getting Becca back. She would tell him the truth when she had her daughter back. She made a silent oath to God then and there that she would tell Buck everything after this was over…whether he wanted to hear it or not.

"Have you eaten? You look tired, Jen. You should stay here tonight."

Her breath caught, her eyes flew to his. That he would offer his home to her only made her deception taste all the more bitter. "No. I wouldn't want to impose."

For all she knew he could have a girlfriend upstairs in bed waiting for him. Or a wife. She hadn't even thought of that. She'd surely have heard about it in the news if he'd gotten married or engaged, but she couldn't be certain.

"I insist that you stay. There's no point in you driving all the way home this late as upset as you are. We'll work this all out in the morning."

He was right.

How on earth could she go home and sleep in her bed knowing her baby wasn't in her room? There was no way she could bear the idea of it, much less the reality. Her daughter's room would be a mess, as usual. Her clothes would be everywhere. The bed unmade. The CD player was probably still jamming with the rap music her daughter had recently acquired a taste for. She forgot to turn it off more often than not in her morning rush to get ready for school. At that point each morning Jenna was usually already in the car warming it up and hoping her daughter would hurry so neither of them would be late. She'd decided that Becca's inability to be ready on time or keep her room clean, as well as the rap music her daughter now liked, were all a result of Jenna paying for the grief she'd given her own parents.

No, she couldn't go home. She couldn't go to her mother. Her mother didn't need this kind of stress with her heart condition. She would not be happy that Jenna had kept this secret, but she had to think of her mother's health. Her friends would only ask questions, questions she didn't want to answer.

There really was no other option.

"I suppose you're right. Thank you."

He stood, leaving her feeling cold and bereft without him next to her—without his strong arm draped around her shoulder. She felt foolish for reacting that way but she was only human.

"I'll show you to one of the guest rooms."

She got up and tried to think what she should say next. It seemed strange to be agreeing to stay in his home when they hadn't seen each other in so many years. They were virtual strangers now. But, if she left, he might have time to ponder her request and decide against helping her. She couldn't take that risk.

"Would you like me to pour you another brandy?"

She shook her head. "No, thank you." Fatigue dragged at her ability to stay vertical. She really was exhausted. She needed to lie down. He'd been right about that, too. She was in no condition to drive home.

"This way." He gestured to the hall. "I'll get you settled and then I'll make a call to Luke Jernigan, the president of the bank. He'll have the money ready as soon as the doors open in the morning."

Hearing him say for sure that he would provide the money made her want to weep. How would she ever repay him? "Thank you, Buck. I can't tell you how much this means to me."

He applied the slightest pressure to the small of her back with his hand, directing her toward the elegant staircase that dominated the entryhall.

"You were going to be a nurse," he commented as they climbed the stairs. "I can see by your scrubs that you did it."

She suddenly felt woozy, and laid a hand on the banister for additional support. "Yes. I'm an E.R. nurse at Jackson County Hospital." She hadn't eaten in more than twelve hours. The one drink had gone straight to her head.

"You're married now?"

She tensed. "No. You?" She wanted to bite her tongue. Why had she asked that?

"No."

The moment felt completely surreal. All this time had passed and here they were chatting as if they'd seen each other just yesterday.

It was dreamlike.

No, it was a nightmare.

Her baby was missing. Pain sliced deep into her heart. If Buck hadn't agreed to help her she had no idea what she would have done. How would she ever thank him, much less pay him back?

He finally stopped in front of an open door. "This one is right across the hall from my room." He motioned to the door behind him. "That way if you need me, all you have to do is call my name. I'm here for you, Jen, whatever you need."

An ache rose in her throat. His gaze met hers and she couldn't help herself. This was too much. How could he say that to her? *Whatever you need...*

"Don't," she said with a shake of her head. God, she felt dizzy. She should have let his remark go.

Confusion lined his face. "I didn't mean to make you uncomfortable, but I meant what I said."

"I need your help, Buck, and I really appreciate it," she admitted, not certain where she was going with this. "I really do. I..." She blinked back the tears. "I don't know what I would have done if you'd said no." She held up a hand when he would have spoken. "But don't pretend the past didn't happen. It did. What you're feeling right now is sympathy. Nothing more. Don't make it seem like it's more."

How could he look at her that way? As if he really did care beyond basic human compassion. As if her words had injured him deeply.

It didn't make sense.

"You're upset," he offered, giving her an out. "We'll talk about all this in the morning."

She let herself look at him, really look for the first time since her arrival. Still tall and broad-shouldered. He was more than a decade older now than when they'd been together, but he'd aged well. The angles and planes of his face were as handsome as ever. The open shirt offered a glimpse of his sinewy chest and the rippled abdomen of a man half his age. He'd stayed fit, which was a lot more than she could say for herself. She worked too many hours, had to rush around far too much for Bec, to worry about staying in shape. But that was part of being a mother.

"You're right." She shouldn't have said all that. Why couldn't she just accept his generosity and keep her mouth shut?

Her eyes met his and in that instant she knew why. Because this man—this man she hadn't seen or spoken to in all those years—still possessed the power to hurt her as no other man on the planet could. And fate had left her no choice but to come to him.

It just wasn't fair.

"I'm sorry," she offered wearily. "I'm just worried, that's all. My baby..." She clamped down on her lower lip a second to stop its trembling. "I can't think straight."

"You don't have to apologize. Get some rest." His eyes searched hers a moment. "Good night, Jen." Then he turned away.

"Good night."

She closed the door to her borrowed room and sagged against it.

All she had to do was get through the next eighteen or so hours without falling apart or making him second-guess his decision.

Surely she could manage that.

CHAPTER FOUR

BUCK STEELED HIMSELF against the bombardment of emotions. Closing his eyes, he tried his level best to block the image of the woman just on the other side of that door.

She was real. She was here.

When he'd found her on his doorstep he'd told himself he had to be dreaming. Maybe he shouldn't have had that last drink. But she was really here.

How was he supposed to act?

He'd pretended the past hadn't happened…just like she said. He'd jumped into the part of Good Samaritan as he would have for any noble cause brought to his attention. That had always been his M.O. What good was all the money if he couldn't help others with it?

But this wasn't just any cause…and he wasn't just playing the part here. He wanted more than anything in this world to take away the pain he'd seen in her eyes. He couldn't bear it.

As if that didn't say enough about his lack of control where she was concerned, once he'd gotten past the initial shock of seeing her, he'd realized one thing with utter clarity. He still wanted her. Maybe he'd never stopped.

She was just as beautiful as before. Her hair was longer, gliding down and around her shoulders like sleek, dark running water. Those blue-gray eyes still made his gut lock with need. The smooth pale skin that refused to be tanned could have been made of the fragilest of porcelain. So soft and delicate…so perfect. But the part that devastated him the most were those lush lips. So full and rich in color. Jenna had never needed lipstick. That mouth was devil-red on the face of an angel.

His mouth watered at the memory of how she tasted—sweet and soft and exhilarating. She'd made him feel as if he was flying whenever they kissed. Making love with her was the only thing in this world that had ever exceeded the rush of barreling past that checkered flag. She was the only woman who'd had the power to make him love her more than he loved racing.

Why hadn't he been able to make her see that? Why in hell had he ever let her get away?

Because he'd been a fool. He should have fought for her. Just because she'd given up and walked away hadn't meant he'd had to.

But he had. He'd let her go, assuming she would come back eventually.

The joke had been on him.

A couple of months had passed, and then a year,

with him climbing to the top as the hottest driver on the circuit. He'd told himself that his work was all that mattered at the time, so he stayed focused on his career and his philanthropic work. He'd convinced himself that if she didn't love him enough to come back that he didn't need her.

But he'd been wrong.

Evidently she'd found someone new to give her what he refused to.

Fury lashed through him, made him want to tear apart with his bare hands the man whose name he didn't even know.

The idea that she'd had a child with another man tightened his jaw, twisted his gut. But what had he expected? She hadn't belonged to him in a very long time. Evidently she had moved on with her life in the fullest meaning of the phrase.

Buck blew out a weary breath of frustration. What did it matter? He would have agreed to give her the money regardless of the reason she needed it. His friends would call him a fool and he'd have to agree. He didn't know her anymore. He didn't even know if she actually had a child…or if her request was anything more than a scam to milk him for the money. But he knew what he felt inside. He rubbed at the ache in his chest.

There were some things a man couldn't control and his heart was one of them.

Maybe it was the guilt he'd always felt for letting

her go so easily. He owed her. He never shirked his responsibilities. Jenna Williams had loved him. She'd been a virgin when they met. She hadn't been the kind of woman to give herself freely. She'd given herself to him with the understanding that it was forever, that he would be the one and only. He'd taken all she had to offer for nearly a year and then he'd simply let her go when things had gotten into territory that scared the hell out of him.

Yeah, he owed her.

He would move heaven and earth in an effort to see that she got her daughter back. Fury detonated inside him all over again. Whoever was torturing Jenna like this would pay. He would see to that as well.

Taking a deep breath and then letting it out slowly, he shook off the questions and emotions gnawing at him. If he was going to help her there were steps he needed to take. Call Jernigan and order the money, even if it was after midnight. While he was at it, just in case, he'd put in a call to Saul Bellamy, his attorney. He didn't exactly want to check up on Jenna, he just wanted to be sure she wasn't in some kind of trouble that had prompted the kidnapping of her daughter.

A precautionary step, he told himself. Or maybe just something to make him feel better in case he turned out to be an even bigger fool than his friends were already going to think he was.

He paused before turning away from her door. Still

silent inside the room. She needed to sleep. He hoped she would manage at least a few hours rest. A muffled sound tugged him closer, had him straining to hear.

Sobbing.

That knot in his gut tightened. He touched the door. It was all he could do not to barge in there, take her in his arms and hold her until she fell asleep. But that would be a mistake. He was operating on emotion here. Somehow he had to get a dose of logic back into this situation.

With monumental effort, he went downstairs. As he reached for the phone on the table next to the sofa, he noticed her purse on the floor. It had fallen over and some of the contents had spilled onto the rug. He crossed to where she'd sat, knelt down and gathered up her things. Her wallet, a few coins, a utility bill and a handful of photographs. He tucked all but the photographs back into her purse.

Curiosity getting the better of him, he stared at the first of the pictures as he pushed to his feet, then the next. A frown furrowed its way across his brow as he shifted to yet another of the photos. All were pictures of Jenna with a girl who looked to be twelve or thirteen. Long brown hair, wide smile. The kid was tall if he'd guessed her age accurately. Tall and rail-thin…vaguely familiar-looking.

Confused, he shuffled through a few more. Was this the child that was missing? It wasn't until he reached the last photo that the epiphany struck.

The final photograph was a close-up of the girl, the same one pictured in every single photo. To go along with that brown hair, she had big brown eyes and a splattering of freckles across her nose. He recognized those freckles. The recognition altered something inside him, something deep, on a fundamental level.

His sister Reba had those same freckles…same brown eyes and hair…so did he. The tall, slender figure was just like his mother's…just like his sister's.

Twelve or thirteen years old…

Shock quaked through him.

How could this be?

This girl was his daughter.

He didn't need Jenna's confirmation or even DNA testing.

He knew.

His movements mindless, he placed the pictures back into her purse. All but one—the close-up. Then he crossed back to the phone.

The idea that some bastard had taken her against her will, was holding her for ransom, filled him with murderous thoughts. If this scumbag harmed a single hair on the child's head—his child's—he would kill him or die trying.

There had to be a mistake. How could Jenna have been pregnant, have raised this child without telling him?

A new kind of rage ignited inside him. She had

some powerful explaining to do. He needed answers. But the memory of how broken and vulnerable she'd looked when he'd opened the door charged into his head, causing his rage to wilt. He couldn't make any demands on her right now. Not until he made right on his promise to help her.

All he wanted was confirmation of a truth she couldn't possibly hope to deny.

Bec's father is out of the picture.

He swallowed with difficulty. *He* was out of the picture. Bec—she'd called the girl *Bec*. Had to be short for Becky or Rebecca. His mother's name had been Rebecca. Reba had been named a variation of Rebecca.

This was too much to take in at once.

He had a child.

A daughter.

Who played soccer.

Who was missing.

The rage sparked once more. He needed backup on this. Buck went to his study and sat down behind the desk, the picture still in his hand. This was something he couldn't talk about on the phone. There were people he needed here, now, to help him make the best decisions. God knew he wasn't thinking exactly straight under the circumstances.

His hand stilled on the phone. Why hadn't she told him? Had she been that angry at him? That disappointed?

A cold, harsh memory trickled through his veins.

He hadn't wanted children.

He'd made that clear time and again.

Since Jenna left the subject hadn't come up…he hadn't allowed himself to get that close to anyone else. The idea of a family hadn't crossed his mind since.

How could he blame her? This was as much his fault as hers. Maybe more.

He shook off the agonizing questions and dialed the first number. His public relations expert answered before the second ring. The entire team knew that calls coming at this hour wouldn't be good.

"Lori, I need you here now."

She assured him she would be right there.

Next on his list was George Farley. Next to Tom McElroy, George knew him better than anyone. George knew Jenna as well, remembered the days when they were together. Buck needed that kind of anchor in all this. Then he called his attorney, Saul Bellamy. Saul was a good man, honest as the day was long and wise beyond his years. With a final call to the bank president Luke Jernigan, there was nothing left to do but wait.

And wonder how things might have been…

By the time everyone had arrived and Buck had relayed the admittedly shocking details it was past 1:00 a.m. When he'd said what he had to say he'd expected a mixed reaction. But he sure as hell hadn't anticipated the silence.

Saul was the first to break the deafening quiet. "But she hasn't confirmed your suspicions," he suggested.

Buck shook his head. "No. She was exhausted when she got here. She needs sleep right now."

Lori surged to her feet and started to pace. She would be worried about the public's reaction to this. That was her job. "So you don't actually know." She fixed her gaze on Buck's, her hands planted solidly on her hips.

His shoulders moved up then down. "I don't have any legal proof." He turned up the intensity in his own gaze to let her see just how certain he was. "But I know. You'd have to be blind not to see it."

"She does look a mite like Reba, that's true," George chimed in. "But the Buchanans don't have the patent on brown eyes and freckles."

Buck couldn't argue with that. But he knew. "I'm not going to debate whether or not she's my daughter. That will be cleared up soon enough. The reason I asked all of you here is so that we can be prepared for whatever goes down in the next twenty-four hours. Right now, I might not be thinking straight enough to make certain decisions."

"As your attorney," Saul spoke up again, "I have to advise you that the proper course of action is to go to the authorities." He flared his hands. "Buck, you're not qualified to deal with a situation like this. None of us are. This could end tragically if we don't take the right steps. Assuming the kidnapping is real."

"If we go to the police, he'll kill the girl." Buck ran a hand through his hair. "It's real." He'd heard Jenna crying behind that closed door. He didn't have all the details, but he knew the fear was real.

Lori huffed a breath of frustration. "Come on, Buck, how do we know there's a kidnapper? No offense to Jenna, but all we've got is her word right now. She could be running a scam on you."

Buck took a moment to tamp down the anger that bolted through him at Lori's words. She was playing devil's advocate here. He got that. But she was wrong. He knew Jenna better than that. Lori did, too. None of them had forgotten how tense things had been those last few months before Jenna left. That was likely playing a role in Lori's attitude. She didn't want Buck hurt again.

Too late.

"You know her, Lori. How can you say something like that?" he argued. It pained him that a member of his team would think so poorly of the woman he'd once loved…still had feelings for. As crazy as it sounded, it was true.

"I knew her thirteen years ago, Buck. I don't know her now and neither do you." Lori turned her palms up, her arms wide apart. "Maybe the child is yours. Maybe Jenna decided it was time for you to pay up."

When Buck would have argued with that thinking, George spoke up again. "Look, Buck, you can't expect us to blindly go with what you're suggesting.

We need proof. We need clarification. Like Lori said, this could turn into a major media circus for the whole team. We're two weeks away from the Daytona. The timing just seems a little convenient."

All valid points.

But he didn't agree, not completely.

"We'll keep this quiet for now," he said, looking from one to the other. "That's necessary. The kidnapper made his demands quite clear. No police. Nothing. Just the money. I don't want a word of this to get out. I want you to keep your eyes and ears open, watch my back on this. We can't take any chances."

"For the record," Saul said, his face grim, "I think you're making a mistake."

JENNA WASHED HER FACE with cold water to help reduce the swelling and redness. She should lie back down and try to sleep. But she couldn't. Not until she'd made this right.

She placed the damp cloth on the sink and went back into the adjoining bedroom. She glanced at the clock. Half past one. Part of her wanted desperately to call her mother, but that would be selfish. There was nothing her mother could do and the worry wouldn't help her heart. She'd just have to bear this alone for now.

Agony roared so abruptly and so violently inside Jenna that she doubled over, hugging herself in an attempt to hold the screams inside. Just when she thought she had pulled it together, reality rattled her again. This couldn't be. Couldn't be.

Who would want to take her baby?

Who would hurt her this way?

It had to be about Buck. She straightened, scarcely able to make her muscles loosen enough for the effort. She ran a trembling hand over her face and wiped the fresh tears from under her eyes. He was right. This was about him and his money. But how had this sick bastard discovered the truth about Buck being Becca's father.

No one knew.

Maybe someone had put the facts together? The time frame of when she'd broken up with Buck fit, if anyone bothered to do the math. She was pretty sure her mother had always suspected but she'd never asked any questions. Her mother knew how badly it hurt to talk about Buck and the breakup. She'd always been there for Jenna and Becca without question, without hesitation. If she learned her beloved grandchild was in danger…

Jenna shuddered, couldn't think about that right now.

Maybe if this was just about the money, maybe Bec would be safe. She wouldn't be of any value to the kidnapper if he harmed her.

The anguish seared through her at the thought. *Please, please, don't let him hurt my girl.*

Pull it together, she told herself. She couldn't think

rationally if she allowed her emotions to rage out of control over and over like this. She had to be strong.

Right now she had to see if Buck was still up and apologize for her behavior. Between the fatigue of working so many hours, failing to eat and…the other, she'd been on the verge of a total collapse when she'd arrived at his door. She needed him to know how very much she appreciated what he was doing. Allowing her bitterness about the past to get in the way was wrong.

She had been struggling to hold it together since receiving that damned call. Not holding back and letting the tears come had helped a little. Surely she could keep her cool now. Once she got this apology off her chest she would actually try for some sleep.

After straightening the scrubs she'd been wearing for going on twenty-four hours as best she could, she finger-combed her hair and went in search of her host. The door to his room was open. He wasn't there.

At the top of the stairs she hesitated and listened. She was sure she heard voices. Careful not to make a sound, she eased down a few more steps. Yes, she definitely heard voices. Buck for one. And…a female voice.

Oh, Lord, he was probably attempting to explain to his girlfriend why he has a strange woman in the house. Well, one look at her and this woman would know she had no competition. Jenna looked and felt like hell. The lady had nothing to worry about.

Another voice drifted up the stairs to greet her, this one male. Vaguely familiar.

Jenna took the final steps down to the entryhall. She listened again to determine from which direction the voices were coming. That big room with the bar, she estimated. Impolite or not, she decided to eavesdrop a little more before making her presence known.

When she reached the double doors that led into the fancy room, she paused. Getting a handle on the situation before she burst into the room was the smart thing to do.

"Before you make any rash decision, Buck, you should get all the facts." The male voice.

She knew that voice. She was almost certain.

"He's right and you know it."

The woman again. Also a familiar voice now that she could hear her better.

"We're not trying to talk you out of what you want to do, Buck." A second male voice. "We simply want you to measure your response to this discovery. Don't jump the gun. Gather the facts and react accordingly. If the girl has been kidnapped, going to the police is the logical next step."

Fear exploded in Jenna's veins.

She'd entered the room before her sluggish brain could catch up and issue the command to react. "You can't do that."

Heads turned and all eyes were suddenly on her.

"He said she would die if we went to the police," Jenna reminded Buck, trying her best to relay the urgency with her eyes and her voice. "You can't go to the police." Her heart thumped so hard she couldn't hear herself think, but she had to get her point across. He couldn't listen to these people.

"Jenna."

Her gaze collided with the woman's and recognition flared. Lori Houser. She was Buck's public relations guru. He was already evaluating the media fallout. Had nothing changed? Fury burned away the fear she'd felt seconds ago. This was about her daughter. She didn't care how it looked or the domino effect in the press.

"What're you doing, Buck?" Jenna let him see the disappointment in her eyes. "You said you'd help me. Do you need your team's permission?"

"Jenna, it's not like that."

She jerked her attention to the man who'd spoken. Oh, yes, she remembered him. George Farley, crew chief. He'd been a nice guy. Back then.

"Then tell me what it's like, George? This is my daughter we're talking about. I know what the kidnapper said. If I go to the police she dies. If I don't give him the money she dies. Sounds clear enough to me." Her pulse skipped at the idea that these people might persuade him not to help her. She couldn't let that happen.

The other man, one she didn't recognize, stood. "Ms. Williams—"

"Wait, Saul." Buck looked from the man who'd

spoken to the others. "We'll continue this discussion tomorrow."

Saul nodded, but he didn't look happy about not being heard.

Jenna held her ground as each one passed her. Lori said nothing. Saul nodded. George was the only one who spoke.

"I'm sure sorry about this, Jenna." And then he left with the rest.

She stared after them, hoping that he meant he was sorry about what had happened to her daughter and not because they'd talked Buck out of helping her.

"Would you like something to eat now?"

She turned back to Buck. He'd buttoned his shirt but it still hung loose from his trousers. Like her, he looked as if he could use some sleep.

"Jenna?"

She snapped back to the present. "Sorry. No. I'm okay." She couldn't possibly eat.

"I'm starved," he said. "Come on to the kitchen and we'll talk. That is if you don't mind watching me eat."

He didn't wait for an answer. She trailed after him, distracting herself with taking in more details of his home. The dining room they passed was enormous and elegant, of course. The kitchen had the professional look of a chef's retreat. Stainless steel and sleek granite. Oversized appliances and endless cabinets. She wondered how often he actually ate in here.

She scooted onto a stool at the island and watched

as he rummaged in the refrigerator until he'd rounded up the essentials for making a club sandwich.

"You didn't tell me your daughter's full name. You called her Bec, I believe." This he said as he slathered the bread with mayo. Then he piled on thinly sliced layers of ham, turkey and cheese.

"Becca." Even saying her name out loud had pain twisting in her belly. She wanted her child home with her. She had to be scared to death. Had to be afraid she'd never see her mother again. Jenna closed her eyes and pushed the horrifying thoughts away. She couldn't bear to think them. Nor could she tell Buck that she'd named her daughter after his mother.

Tomato slices and lettuce topped the mound of meat and cheese before he placed the final slice of bread on top. He took a big bite and groaned in appreciation. She watched him chew, her stomach reacting with a different kind of pang this time. This one clearly related to the fact she hadn't eaten in fourteen or so hours.

"This is really good. Why don't you let me fix one for you?" His brown eyes studied her intently, the concern there real. "I know you must be hungry."

She licked her lips, considered whether or not she could actually swallow anything with the emotion lodged in her throat. "I'll try," she surrendered. She did need to keep up her strength. This was going to be a long day.

He piled on the layers, making her a sandwich

exactly like his own except with mustard instead of mayo. How did he remember that about her?

"There you go." He pushed the plate toward her. "Milk? Tea?"

"Milk is fine."

She took a tentative bite as he poured a glass of milk. It tasted wonderful but getting it down wasn't exactly easy. The second bite went down a little more smoothly.

They ate in silence for a minute or two. It was almost like old times. Only he'd lived in a smaller house and they'd both been a lot younger. They would make love for hours and then raid his fridge. Most of the time they would end up making love again…on the table or the kitchen counter…of course it had been Formica then.

She shivered, pushing the memories away. That had been a long time ago.

Jenna had to stop plunging back into the past. She could feel the tension mounting, growing heavier with each second that passed. His friends had hauled him back to reality. Had probably called her a gold-digger. Had likely warned him to be wary of what she was really up to. She could just imagine all the less-than-nice things they'd had to say about her. But she also fully understood that they were simply trying to protect Buck. They were his friends.

"I guess they still don't like me."

Her breath hitched and her eyes rounded at the idea that she'd actually said the words. She hadn't meant to say that out loud.

He parked the remainder of his sandwich on his plate and flattened his hands on the cool granite counter. "Jenna, they're worried about you and your daughter."

"And you," she countered, setting her own sandwich aside. She knew the deal. She'd always been seen as an outsider. He could paint it anyway he wanted to, but she knew. "I'm sure Lori warned you against getting involved with me and my troubles considering the repercussions if the media was to get hold of it."

Those penetrating brown eyes leveled on hers. "That's Lori's job. It doesn't mean she isn't concerned about the welfare of your little girl."

"And Saul, who was he?" He was the one unknown factor. She hadn't seen him before.

"He's my attorney."

Her pulse scrambled. "Your attorney? Why did you think you needed to talk to your attorney?"

He searched her eyes before he answered, looking long and hard as if he needed to find something only he could name or would recognize when he encountered it. "This is a very dangerous situation, Jenna. We needed advice not motivated by emotion. Saul pointed out a number of things you and I might overlook."

"Like what?" A new kind of tension stole into her, made her want to run. But she couldn't come up with the money any other way.

"Like the fact that whoever took Becca might be angling for more than just the ransom money."

"No." She shook her head, refused to consider that concept. "He asked for the money. That's all."

"He'll get the money. I don't want you worrying about that."

She relaxed—marginally.

"But before we go any further, I need *all* the facts."

Fear crashed against her already unsteady composure. "I don't know what you mean. I told you everything I know."

He reached into his shirt pocket and pulled out a photograph. He placed it on the counter. Jenna's heart squeezed. Becca's big brown eyes stared up at her…her breathtaking smile…those precious freckles.

"Start with the truth, Jenna."

Her gaze lifted to his as that fear and uncertainty was joined by dread.

"Is this little girl my daughter?"

CHAPTER FIVE

THIS WAS THE MOMENT she'd dreaded since recognizing that Buck was her only hope. He'd promised to help her, no questions ask. And now suddenly he wanted all the facts—he wanted answers.

Why did it matter?

"You said you'd help me, Buck." She braced herself for the fury she knew would come. Buck Buchanan had always been an easygoing guy. It took a heck of a lot to make him mad, but one of the things she remembered vividly about him was just how much he despised duplicity of any sort. "Will my answer change your decision about the money?"

He looked away.

She hoped that she could still count on his word. That his reputation for never, ever going back on his word hadn't changed. He'd lived by the motto that a man was only as good as his word. Please, please let that still be the case.

His gaze swung back to hers. "You know it won't. The money is yours no matter your answer. But I need the truth." He moved a step closer and searched her face with clear desperation in his eyes. "The whole truth."

"Why were you looking through my purse?" she hedged, barely resisting the urge to lean back. The photos had been in her purse. She'd brought them for him—before changing her mind about telling him he had a daughter. He had no right prowling through her things. Her question would only delay the inevitable, but that was fine by her.

Frustration tightened his square jaw. "You dropped your purse, I guess. It was lying on its side and the pictures had spilled out. I didn't look in your purse," he said pointedly. "You're avoiding my question."

Big breath. "Yes, Buck. She's your biological child. Satisfied?"

Maybe she shouldn't have snapped, but she had over thirteen years of bitterness tucked away and whenever the subject came up a little of it reared its ugly head.

"Good Lord." He plowed a hand through his hair.

She'd expected the news to shock him, maybe even make him angry, but she hadn't anticipated this mixture of misery and defeat. The way she'd seen this going was her admitting the truth and him lashing out in startled fury. After all, he hadn't wanted any children. Frankly, she didn't see why he would care that she hadn't told him. Besides, he'd kept things from her when they'd first met. Turnabout was fair play.

Just when she thought he couldn't say or react in a way that would surprise her more, he did.

"Did you hate me that much?"

The sincerity in his eyes wouldn't let her take his words for anything other than what they were—genuine.

"No." She shook her head adamantly, emotional overload preventing her from maintaining a reasonable hold on her outward composure. She'd never hated him. Not even after leaving when she'd been so lonely without him and so miserable. "My decision had nothing to do with hating you."

An inkling of that anger she'd expected made an appearance. "Then why? Why would you keep this from me? Didn't you think I had a right to know?"

Here they went. The blame game. The blowup. She couldn't handle this right now. Couldn't he understand that? Her daughter was missing. Her child was in grave danger. She didn't want to argue with him.

She dragged in a deep, bolstering breath and let it out slowly in hopes of putting the brakes on the emotions attempting to run even wilder. "I made the decision. At the time it felt like the right thing to do since you told me from the beginning that you weren't interested in children. Remember?" She looked straight into his eyes, and saw the hurt and the anger there. "I'm sorry if I hurt you, but…" She worked her throat in an effort to swallow back the tears that gathered. "Right now it's all I can do to hold it together. I can't get into a debate on the subject."

The anger vanished, leaving only the pain, and a glimmer of the defeat she'd seen moments before.

"I wish you'd given me the chance to make that decision for real." He closed his eyes and let go a heavy breath of his own. "But you're right, when we have her safely back, we'll hash this out."

That was fair. "I appreciate that."

"We should both get some sleep," he suggested. "This is going to be a long day."

She was reasonably sure that sleep wouldn't be coming anytime soon, but he was right. She had to try. The last few hours had already been the longest of her life. It was doubtful that the next few would be any better.

"I need to get my cell phone charger from my car." It was a miracle she'd thought of it after what happened. But somehow she'd known that her only connection with the kidnapper was her phone. Keeping it charged and operational was essential.

"I'll walk out with you."

Relief made her knees a little weak as she followed Buck out the front door. She'd made it past two hurdles. He now knew that Bec was his daughter and she'd faced the team. At least certain key members of the team. She found it odd that Tom McElroy hadn't come. He and Buck had been practically inseparable. Maybe he was out of town on business. Guys like Tom and Buck stayed out of town a lot. Part of the job. She was extremely lucky Buck had been home tonight.

At her car she opened the driver's side door and reached across to the passenger seat where she'd flung the charger. She wondered if Bec's phone was fully charged. As she straightened out of the car and closed the door, she wondered if her daughter had eaten. If she were asleep. Had the bastard who'd taken her been mean to her…had he hurt her in any way?

Her body began to shake despite her valiant efforts to restrain the violent shudders at all the unanswered questions. She couldn't bear to consider the idea that he might have hurt her…touched her in some sick, evil way. *Please, God, keep my baby safe.*

By the time she reached the front door of Buck's house again she couldn't hide the quaking.

His arm went around her, steadied her. "She's going to be fine," he promised gently. "This scumbag wants money. I'm certain he understands that his power lies in the viability of the asset he now controls. He won't do anything to jeopardize the negotiability of that asset."

Jenna told herself he was right. That it was about the money and whoever had done this had planned well. He'd gone to a lot of trouble to find a way to extort money from Buck. This had to be about Buck.

And here she'd thought she had protected her daughter from this very possibility by keeping her father's name a secret—even Becca's birth certificate said *Father Unknown.*

So much for keeping secrets.

She understood that there were people who made it their mission in life to dig up negotiable information on celebrities. Buck Buchanan fit neatly into that category. Someone had put two and two together and figured it out, that was all. Jenna hadn't ever been married. The timeline fit with when she'd broken up with Buck.

That had to be the answer.

"I keep telling myself that he won't hurt her, that he only wants the money." She stared up at Buck. "Thank you for reinforcing that." The quaking settled a little more.

He walked her to the guestroom, and kept his arm firm around her, providing the strength she desperately needed just now.

Funny, she realized, as he said good-night and closed the door, she'd never expected it to be this way. There hadn't really been any doubt in her mind as to whether or not he would help her. But this calm reassurance was surreal. Where was the explosion of outrage that she would dare keep his child from him? The threat to take her to court regarding custody when this was over? Despite the fact that he had steadfastly proclaimed he didn't want any children, he would never shun his responsibilities. He would see this as a responsibility he had not been able to meet, which amounted to neglect in his eyes.

As reasonably calm as he appeared to be right now, Jenna had a bad feeling that the explosion was yet to come.

BUCK DIDN'T GO to his room once he'd left Jenna in the guestroom. Instead he went back downstairs and collapsed on the sofa. He picked up the picture of the little girl and stared at the sweet features of her face.

How could he have a twelve-year-old daughter and not have known it?

Because he'd sworn he would never go down that road. He would not risk that he would be responsible for letting down a kid of his own. The best way to ensure that didn't happen was not to have any. He and Jenna had been so careful he wasn't even sure how this had happened. Right now she was in no shape for him to even ask.

He set his elbows on his knees, pressed his fingertips to his forehead and rubbed at the tension there. His old man had been a worthless drunk who beat his wife and kids regularly. He'd disappeared when Buck was nine. Even at that young age he remembered what his mother had suffered in order to support two kids. That hard life and all the worry had helped to put her in an early grave. But he and Reba had managed to not only survive, but to thrive. He'd jumped into the business of stock car racing, first as a member of the pit crew, then as a driver and eventually a team owner. Extreme focus had ensured his success. And he'd never failed to show proper appreciation for those who helped him get there, including his team.

But his personal life had suffered. He couldn't

deny that. Nor could he deny having wondered from time to time what it would be like to have a family— wife, kids, the whole nine yards. But the bad memories had kept him firm on his stance not to drag kids into his hectic lifestyle. Hell, Jenna had left him because she felt cheated by his dedication to racing. How would a kid feel?

Too late to fret over that now.

How could he have been this oblivious to the woman he'd supposedly loved thirteen years ago? He'd allowed her to walk away. She hadn't wanted to be with him anymore. She'd been tired of the life of racing. He'd let it go at that.

Well, he hadn't actually let it go, but he'd left it alone. He'd never told a soul except Tom that he still loved her. His old buddy had insisted that things were better the way they had turned out. Jenna hadn't understood, hadn't wanted to fit into who Buck was on the track. Tom had told Buck he might be miserable with her as a wife.

The thought of Tom McElroy had ire churning in his gut. All those years he'd thought of Tom as a brother and the SOB had betrayed him. Stupid jealousy had driven him to try and damage the career of their team's driver, Rush Jackson. For reasons Buck might never fully understand, Tom had wanted Rush out of the picture. As manager of the Rocket City Racers, he'd hurt the whole team with his attempts to bring down their winning driver. Leaking

DEBRA WEBB79

untruths and doctored photographs that could have jeopardized the team's relationship with sponsors as well as fans. Bad, bad business.

Buck had fired him and McElroy understood that NASCAR backed Buck's decision.

He touched the face in the photo. His child. Unbelievable. And already he'd failed her. He'd missed her first steps, her first words, her first day of school. Everything. She was practically a teenager. She probably wouldn't want anything to do with him.

Did she even know who he was?

He glanced toward the entryhall and briefly considered going upstairs to ask Jenna that suddenly important question. But she needed to get some sleep. No need to upset her again. The toll this was taking on her was unfathomable. He'd only just learned that the girl was his and already he wanted to rant and curse at the mere thought of some sick bastard hurting her. He recognized it as the most basic part of human compassion. This was *his* child. He stared at the photo. His flesh and blood.

That knowledge made everything different... every single thing.

He had to get Becca back. Safe and sound. No matter the cost.

He leaned his head back and closed his eyes. How had he let her get away? They'd been so in love. Or so he'd thought. Sure, there had been problems. Jenna hadn't enjoyed his commitment to the sport he loved. Racing was who he was as much as it was what he did.

He hadn't exactly lied to Jenna, but, like her, he hadn't been honest with her all those years ago.

His appendix had ruptured. The warning signs that trouble was afoot had been there, but he'd ignored the pain until emergency surgery had been necessary. No one on the team had wanted the media to find out about the illness so close to the kickoff of a new season. The fix had been simple. Take him to a hospital in another county under an alias. No big deal.

Buck just hadn't expected to meet Jenna there. She'd been in college at the time and working at the hospital had put money in her pocket, as well as pro- viding a couple of extra credits toward her degree program. He'd ended up staying ten days due to the infection caused by his ignoring the problem. Ten days was all it had taken. He'd fallen for the sweet little nurse's aide and she'd fallen for him.

She hadn't known a thing about NASCAR or stock car racing. That should have been a red flag, but he had ignored the warnings. By the time their relationship had ended, he'd realized that there were just some things he couldn't fight. She didn't under- stand or appreciate the thing he loved most besides her—racing.

Jenna was the first and only woman to steal his heart.

He'd known that getting involved that deeply at

such a pivotal time in his career had come with its own set of risks, but he'd been willing to take the chance. He was a race car driver. He took risks all the time on the track. He'd wanted her that badly. Still, he'd failed. Their lives had been too different, their priorities a world apart.

She'd walked away and he'd gone on to the top. Had hovered there for seven straight years, then he'd left driving behind and used his victory money to become a team owner. A lot of people hadn't understood why he'd made that decision, not even his so-called friend McElroy. But he'd needed the change. Something had been missing. Building the Rocket City Racers had filled that emptiness for a time. Then, lately, he'd started to feel that hollowness again.

It didn't make sense.

He'd wondered as recently as the past twenty-four hours if his choice not to dive into another deep relationship, to avoid marriage and definitely fatherhood, had finally caught up to him. He'd kicked that concept aside. Blamed his melancholy on his long-time friend's betrayal. But it had gone deeper than that.

Now he discovered he had a child and fate had to go and deal him a hand like this.

He opened his eyes and sat forward again, his gaze going automatically to the picture of his daughter.

How the hell was he supposed to fix this?

Jenna had made a choice to leave him out of his daughter's life. Would she even be receptive to his involvement now? Would he only screw things up worse than they already were?

Frustration spiked. That was one issue upon which he intended to stand firm. He had a daughter. He would know his daughter and she would know him, no matter the choice Jenna had made or how bone-headed he'd been in the past. Everything had changed now, Jenna would have to get used to that.

The grandfather clock in the hall chimed then counted the hour. 3:00 a.m. He needed to sleep. Whatever happened next he needed to be on his toes. Sleep was necessary.

He couldn't call Reba at this hour. Though he wanted to share this with his sister, he needed to have a better grasp on what was going on first.

Just go to bed, he ordered as he picked up the photograph. This one he intended to keep. Fatigue slowing his step, he climbed the stairs and trudged to his room. He stopped at Jenna's door and started to check on her but changed his mind. He might disturb her. He didn't want that. Instead he stood there thinking about how it used to be.

He flattened his hand on the closed door and con-sidered how truly astonishing this entire night had been. He'd ached for her so many times and now she was here. She'd carried his child in that beautiful body…raised his little girl. He didn't have to ask to know that she'd dedicated herself completely to the child. The smile on the girl's face said it all. She was happy and well-loved. Jenna had not failed as a mother.

He was the one who'd failed.

Giving himself grace, she hadn't exactly given him an opportunity to do otherwise.

He turned away from her door, told himself to slow down. He hadn't seen her in over thirteen years. A lot could have changed. He was giving her the benefit of every doubt. Maybe that wasn't so smart. His friends would certainly agree with that supposition. But until he had reason not to, he intended to take her at her word.

That was the best course of action.

After propping the picture against the lamp on his bedside table, he shed his clothes and climbed into bed.

He had a daughter.

Becca, Jenna had called her.

Soccer. He knew that much about her. She played soccer and she was beautiful.

Whoever the dirtbag holding her hostage, he should be afraid. He should be very afraid. When Buck got his hands on him, he would wish he'd never taken a second look at a brown-haired little girl with freckles sprinkled across her nose like faerie dust.

JENNA PACED THE FLOOR at Buck's house the next morning. It was 9:05 a.m. He'd left twenty-five minutes ago. The bank president had called and said the money was ready for pickup. He'd promised to be back as quickly as possible.

She shouldn't be so anxious. The call wasn't supposed to come in until this evening, but she just couldn't be still.

Her daughter had spent the night in the clutches of a stranger, a demented scumbag whose greed far outweighed his compassion. Had she had breakfast this morning? Was she warm? It was awfully cold outside. What if he was keeping her someplace where there was no heat?

Jenna pressed her fingers hard against her temples and tried not to think those things. She needed to focus on what she could do, not what she couldn't even guess. But it was so hard. Her entire being ached for her child. How could this have happened?

Because she'd once been involved with Buck Buchanan.

The possibility that she should have gone to the police in the first place haunted her. But she'd been too afraid to ignore the kidnapper's demands. He'd said he would be watching, monitoring her calls.

She didn't know how that could happen, but she had to believe it was. Could the average everyday Joe get his hands on that kind of technology so easily? She supposed so. With the Internet providing endless possibilities, a person could buy just about anything these days. She would be smart to conclude that this man was not only intelligent but resourceful.

She wanted her daughter back. Now.

Waiting for that call was like dying a thousand times.

She needed a distraction. Exploring Buck's house seemed like as good a way to occupy her time as any. Since she was in the great room, she started there.

Surveying the framed photos, she looked for any female face she didn't recognize. He'd assuredly had girlfriends or maybe even a fiancée since their time together. But she found no pictures to document the theory. Lots of shots of his mom, who had died years ago, his sister and, of course, the team. A number of publicity shots in Victory Lane and candid photos of the whole team with the No. 86 car.

She moved through the massive dining room and the enormous kitchen that she'd already seen. She wandered through the rest of the downstairs, the small family room or keeping room right off the kitchen and a richly paneled study. Upstairs were several bedrooms, each with its own bath. The landscape outside was lovely even in the dead of winter and the lake view was nothing short of spectacular.

If she'd stayed with Buck, she and Bec would be living here now.

But the fancy house wouldn't have made up for his lack of attention. As much as she appreciated what he was doing for her and Becca this morning, he made a far better friend than a potential husband.

The roar of engines and the cry of the announcer echoed from her memory banks, reminding her of all those times she'd had to wait. She had wandered through the rows of brightly colored trailers covered with sponsors' names and drivers' faces until she'd found the one sporting Buck Buchanan's handsome mug. She'd bought a few souvenirs just to be supportive. The energy vibrating from the crowd of fans who had come to immerse themselves in NASCAR culture had felt awesome even to someone who had no real love of the sport. Even she had gotten caught up in the thrill—in the beginning.

Female fans would stand in line for hours to get an autograph. The tailgate parties were taken to the extreme, and fans of no other sport did it quite so well. All of it was overwhelming and apparently contagious to the masses. Yet, somehow she'd always felt a little separate—she was there but not a part of the festivities.

She would watch Buck from afar as he signed autograph after autograph, and posed for hundreds of pictures with fans. He never grew impatient, never grew tired. She loved that about him. He would stand there in that driving suit all the women found so sexy and be "Buck," the high-octane man of their dreams, for as long as required. He was that dedicated.

She couldn't say she didn't see the attraction. The combination of speed and anticipation was exhilarating. No question. Just being close to the track created a huge rush. Standing on Pit Row, she would watch the cars plunge into that first lap and suddenly Buck's car would go past in a blur and the sensation would take her breath away. His skill on the track combined with his showmanship before and after the race was the stuff that legends were made of.

But legends cast enormous shadows and somehow she'd always felt lost in the dark. Just a few minutes in his presence around his friends even now and it was crystal clear that nothing had changed.

At his age she doubted change would be coming.

The connection that yesterday had been his birthday suddenly barreled into her with enough momentum to have her swaying on her feet.

Buck had turned forty.

How could he still be single?

She had an excuse. She'd been busy raising Bec.

He had no excuse.

It just didn't make sense. Maybe he wanted to stay unattached so that his focus on racing wouldn't be splintered. She would lay odds on that scenario.

Standing in the entryhall, she turned around and stared up at the glittering chandelier slung from the two-story-high ceiling. This house was huge. As beautiful as the place was, surely he got lonely from time to time.

Like she did.

He couldn't possibly enjoy being here all alone.

She had to stop analyzing Buck's life and she definitely knew better than to dwell on the past. She returned to the great room and resumed her tedious pacing. She glanced at the clock again. 9:30 a.m. How much longer?

She clutched her cell phone in her hand, considered dialing Bec's number. But that might set off the guy holding her hostage. Another risk she couldn't bear to take. She had to wait. Had to play by his rules.

The choice was not her own.

She wished she'd had clean clothes to put on this morning, but she'd come dressed just as she was, in those pink scrubs she'd worn for what had ended up being a fifteen-and-a-half-hour shift. A change of clothes had been the furthest thing from her mind before heading to Buck's.

When she went home she could shower and change. She assumed they would take the money to her house to wait. It seemed like the logical thing to do. She'd been in Scottsboro when he called before. He'd kidnapped her daughter from her school in Scottsboro.

But then, she hadn't a clue where he might decide to have them drop the money. Maybe it was better to stay here. If the kidnapper knew she'd come to Buck, maybe the drop point would be closer to this location.

No way to know until he called.

Hours and hours from now.

Part of her wanted to check in with her mother, but she couldn't chance breaking down and telling her what was really going on. She'd forced herself to answer her mother's call last night before she'd left for Buck's. Her mother had wanted to know if Jenna had found Becca. She'd assured her mother that ev-

erything was fine but she wasn't at all sure she could
do that again. Jenna looked at the clock again. Dance
practice would start soon. Bec had never missed a
single practice.

The slam of a vehicle door jerked her attention to
the front windows. She rushed over to see who had
arrived. Buck's SUV was parked out front.

Her breath grew shallow and too rapid as she
waited for him to come inside and confirm he had the
money. If he didn't, she didn't know what she was
going to do. Go crazy for sure.

He walked into the house, briefcase in hand.

She stared at him expectantly.

"I have it."

Another of those knee-buckling surges of relief
rushed over her. Thank God.

All they had to do now was wait for the call.

CHAPTER SIX

Buck decided to drive Jenna to Scottsboro and wait. He'd recognized that the waiting was killing her a little bit at a time. At least being at home she could take solace in the familiarity. He just couldn't bear to watch the devastation claim her inch by inch.

By eleven they were at her home and she seemed to relax immediately.

"How long have you lived here?"

Buck surveyed the small white frame house as they emerged from his SUV. Pansies bloomed in the window boxes and a boxwood hedge skirted the little house with green.

The house didn't have a garage but there was a narrow carport just big enough for that old Bug she drove. The same car she'd had when they were together. He'd ridden in the damned little thing once or twice. She'd been as proud of it as if it were a Cadillac.

"I bought the place as soon as I graduated college and got a job." She jammed the key into the lock. "About ten years ago."

So Becca had grown up in this house.

"You lived with your mom before that?"

She pushed the door open and glanced back at him. "Yes."

Having her mother to help with the baby while she finished school would have been a real blessing. He couldn't help wishing she'd given him the chance to help. But then, he'd never given her a reason to think he'd be interested.

Inside the house was neat and cozy with lots of framed photographs. The urge to inspect each one was abruptly overwhelming.

"May I?" He gestured to the photographs.

She nodded. "I need a shower and change of clothes." She stared at the cell phone she'd kept in her hand even when driving. "I know he isn't supposed to call for a while yet, but will you hold onto this?"

"Sure." He held out his hand. Watching her place that phone in his hand was like seeing her cut open her chest and pull out her heart to give to him.

As she started to turn away, he touched her arm. Even that tiny connection made him ache to hold her and somehow reassure her. "We're going to get her back."

She didn't turn around. "Thank you, Buck." She pulled free of his hold and disappeared into the hall beyond the living room.

He picked up first one framed photo, then another, taking his time to really look at each. Most showed

Becca in dance costumes. Ballet, he recognized, the others he wasn't quite sure about. The pictures went all the way back to when she was just a toddler. The girl had been dancing her whole life.

He placed the final photo back on its shelf and rubbed his eyes with the heels of his hands. His hands came away damp. Along with the goofy grin he'd been wearing as he looked at all those frames of memory, emotion had gotten the better of him. He couldn't remember the last time he'd shed any tears. When his mom died, he supposed. The urge to break down had hit him once or twice when Jenna left. He'd felt shattered, out of sorts in most every respect. But she'd chosen to pick up and go in the middle of the racing season and his commitments had given him something to hang onto.

He could hear the blow dryer going now. She'd be out soon. Curiosity got the better of him, prompting him to explore a little more of the house. The kitchen was scarcely big enough for a table and chairs crowded next to a window. A colorful mix of tulips had sprouted from their bulbs in an oversized glass vase on the window ledge. Nearly every square inch of the fridge was covered in Becca's artwork or schedules related to school, dance or soccer.

He felt his lips slide back into that idiotic grin as he admired the girl's ability to create a right decent drawing. The one image that really got to him was the one labeled "My Family." This one looked to be several years old. She'd drawn her mother and herself with their little house in the background. The mother and daughter figures were holding hands. He wondered if this particular piece had hung in the classroom before being brought home. Had Becca felt different because her picture didn't have a father figure represented? Had any of the other kids ever made fun of her for not having a father in her life? He'd sure as hell endured his share of ribbing at having his drunken old man desert him. The idea that she might have endured something similar gnawed at his gut, made him want to grind his teeth.

He'd have to ask Jenna about that.

As if the thought had summoned her, she appeared at the kitchen door. He shifted his attention to her and his breath stopped short of his lungs. It wasn't that she had dressed in anything provocative or fancy, just faded jeans and a pale blue sweater. The part that took his breath was the way the jeans and the sweater fit. They molded to her slim figure, clung to her womanly shape. The blue of the sweater brought out the blue in her eyes and showcased that long black hair hanging around her shoulders.

She was beautiful. Maybe even more beautiful now than she'd been before.

"Feel better now?" He didn't know how he managed to croak out the words, but somehow he did.

"A little." She moved to the fridge. "Would you like something to drink?"

He shook his head. "I was just admiring Becca's artwork."

She studied the pictures held against the fridge with magnets that ranged from letters of the alphabet to hearts and animals. "She's a good student." Jen glanced back at him. "She makes the honor roll every time. She works hard."

When Jenna had poured herself a glass of iced tea, she led the way back to the living room.

"Tell me about her dancing," he said as he took the seat opposite the sofa where she settled.

Jenna smiled as she cradled her glass. "That's her big dream. She loves to dance." Her eyes seemed to light up the more she talked. "She's really good, too. She's won lots of trophies. Juilliard is her goal after high school."

"That's in New York, right?"

Jenna nodded. "And extremely expensive."

"That won't be an issue," he said flatly.

Jenna stared at her glass. "This…" She took a deep breath. "This is going a little fast, Buck. You haven't even met Becca yet. The last time we talked about this kind of thing you didn't even want kids."

He leaned forward, wanted to be closer somehow, but the coffee table stood between them and moving next to her on the sofa would be too much.

"That was then, this is now. She's my daughter. Whatever she needs, I want her to have."

That blue-gray gaze met his, determination glittered there. "She's *my* daughter. I make the decisions in her life. That's not going to change just because you know the truth and you've suddenly decided that being a father might be a nice hobby."

A cold, hard knot of volatile emotions formed in his stomach and even before he asked, he knew the answer. "Does she know I'm her father?"

"No."

The anger swelled in his chest, making it difficult to breathe. "She has no idea?"

Jenna shook her head. "None."

He closed his eyes, couldn't bear to look at the resolution in her expression. She felt no guilt for that fact. He wanted to demand to know what she'd been thinking, keeping his child from him. But he knew the answer to that one.

"She has asked a few times."

His eyes opened to her once more. This time he saw the glimmer of uncertainty in hers.

"I told her that her father was on the road a lot and too busy for us. She accepted that."

So that was how she saw him, saw the relationship they'd shared.

He clasped his hands between his knees and gentled his tone so that what he was about to say didn't come off as combative. "You didn't give me a chance to be anything else, Jen."

She set her glass on the table in front of her and wrapped her arms around her middle. The uncertainty in her eyes had mounted but he couldn't call what he saw guilt.

"I did what I thought was right." Her gaze leveled on his. "I still believe I did the right thing and I won't debate that with you. Now or ever."

Well, at least he had the whole picture. She didn't feel guilty that she had chosen not to tell him about his daughter, or her daughter about him. What on earth could he have done to make her feel that way? Yeah, he'd insisted that he didn't want kids, but people changed. Hadn't he deserved the opportunity to decide? Sure he'd been dedicated to his work, maybe more so than the average NASCAR driver, but he'd been there for her. He'd loved her, by God. How could she pretend he hadn't?

The rage started to build but he squashed it then and there. She was under enough pressure. This debate, as she called it, could wait until this was over.

"Would it be all right if I saw her room?"

The stark pain he saw in Jen's eyes made him wish he could take back the request.

She moistened her lips, drawing his attention to that full, rich mouth. "Sure."

She stood and led the way.

The door was closed and a sign read, "Keep Out."

One hand on the knob, Jenna glanced up at him. "That's new. Evidently teenage hormones have kicked in already."

He produced a smile. "I'll bet she's got a hell of a temper when she gets riled up."

Jenna considered his comment a moment before she responded. "It takes a lot to make her angry, but she gets pretty fired up when she's had enough." Her gaze collided fully with his. "Just like you."

She opened the door and the smell of lilacs filled his nostrils.

"She's big into linen sprays and body sprays," Jenna noted for his benefit. "Everything has to smell good. Right now it's all about lilacs."

A twin-size bed with an iron headboard held center stage in the room. Posters of dancers and shelf after shelf filled with trophies lined the lavender walls. All sorts of embellishments designed for hair decorated what looked like wire trees on a small white dresser. Makeup filled a silver tray.

"The makeup is for recitals and competition. She doesn't wear it to school." Jenna picked up a big makeup brush and touched its soft bristles. "Maybe next year a little blush and mascara."

The closet door stood open and Buck felt reasonably certain the girl didn't want for clothing or shoes.

The bed was heaped with stuffed animals.

A framed photo sitting atop the bedside table drew him there. Becca and three other girls her age. He picked it up, examined the happy faces. "Her friends?"

Jen joined him. "Carrie, Jane and Sasha. They're inseparable."

Buck carefully placed the picture back in its place. "You haven't told anyone, not even your mother?"

Jenna moved her head side to side, the worry and sadness filling her eyes to brimming once more. "Mom had a heart attack last year. I don't want to stress her."

"I'm sorry to hear about her heart." Though Jen's mother hadn't exactly been one of his fans, he sure hated to learn about her ill health. He wondered if she knew that he was Becca's father. "Does she…know?"

Jen touched her daughter's face in the photo. "At first I couldn't talk about it. She didn't ask but she's no fool. Doing the math would have given her the answer. Later, it just didn't seem important anymore."

Not important. Wow. He really had fallen to the bottom of her food chain. This, he feared, was going to be a long, uphill battle.

Jenna's full attention settled back on him then. "I'm sorry if this sounds hurtful, Buck. But this is something you need to think long and hard about. Becca's life, until now, has been very happy with no upheavals or dramatics. Once this is over, I don't want her to be hurt or upset."

"What exactly are you saying, Jenna?"

There was that fierce determination in her eyes once more. "I don't want you making her fall in love with you and then, when the novelty of being a father wears off, discovering that you really don't have time for her."

He refused to let the anger fuel his response. "Is

that the way you saw our relationship?" He was proud of himself for asking the question so calmly when a battle was raging inside him. He'd taken all the remarks in stride so far but even he had his limits.

"It's not how I saw it, Buck. It's the way it was."

She gave him her back and walked out of her daughter's room. Eventually he followed. He gave himself a minute or two to get a better grip on his composure. They had several more hours before the kidnapper would call. They had to stay focused on the real goal. Nothing else mattered.

Jenna stood in the living room near the window that looked out over the neat little yard, her arms folded around her. As he watched, her shoulders shook ever so slightly. She was working hard to maintain her composure. The bitter words she flung at him were encouraged in part by her fear. He had to keep that in mind.

He moved up behind her, dared to rest his hands on her shoulders, mostly because he couldn't resist the temptation to touch her. That she tensed at his touch was like a kick in the gut. He didn't know why he expected any other kind of reaction, but, foolishly, somehow he had.

"You should eat something, Jen. I know you don't have an appetite, neither do I, but we won't be as sharp mentally if we don't take care of the essentials." He'd learned that after years of driving at speeds of one hundred and eighty miles per hour.

No matter how excited you got, no matter that the adrenaline stole one's hunger, maintaining that necessary unbreakable focus required that sugar levels were kept stabilized. Fuel for the body was absolutely essential for peak reaction times, as well as stamina.

"I usually go grocery shopping on Saturdays." She shrugged. "Maybe we can find something."

"There's always PB and J," he teased gently. They'd often thrived on peanut butter and jelly sandwiches in the middle of the night after hours of lovemaking.

She turned to face him, scarce inches separating them. "I don't know how I feel about this, Buck," she confessed, that haunting desperation back in her eyes now. "I don't know how we'll come to terms with having you in our lives. But the one thing I know with complete certainty is that things will never be like they were before. I can't go back to that."

He let her escape to the kitchen alone, took his time, didn't join her until she'd already smeared peanut butter and jelly onto bread and poured glasses of milk. Just like old times…*almost*.

They ate in silence. He imagined the food was about as tasteless for her as it was him. But the act was necessary.

The cell phone lying on the table between them burst into sound, sending a sharp stab of fear deep into his chest.

Jenna stared at him, then the phone.

As if in slow motion she reached out and picked it up, studying the caller ID.

"It's him."

The words were barely a whisper and yet screaming with terror.

He took hold of her free hand, dragging her attention to him. "Be calm. Listen carefully. Tell him you have what he wants."

She nodded then opened the phone. "Hello."

For several endless seconds she listened. Her gaze collided with Buck's. She held the phone out to him. "He wants to speak with you."

Obviously this bastard was monitoring their movements. Buck accepted the phone and pressed it to his ear. "This is Buchanan." Fury whipped through him and it was all he could do not to tell this piece of crap exactly what he intended to do to him once he got his hands on him.

"Listen carefully, Buchanan," the voice snarled. "Your daughter's life depends solely upon your actions at this point."

Buck's jaw clenched to hold back the words he wanted so desperately to utter. The voice was just as Jenna had described it, garbled. Whoever was making the call was using a scrambler to camouflage that aspect of his identity.

"Since you appear to be ready now, I see no need to wait until the agreed-upon time."

"We're ready," Buck confirmed. "I have the money."

"Very good. At precisely one o'clock you are to drive to Unclaimed Baggage. I'm sure you know the place."

"Yes, I know the store."

"Walk inside alone with the briefcase in hand. Go straight to the upper level on your right and leave the briefcase in the area where luggage is sold. Then leave. Get in your car and drive away. If you hesitate, if you fail to make the drop exactly as I say, *your* child will die."

"I understand."

"Once the drop has been made and the contents of the briefcase confirmed, I will call this number and provide the location of the child. She will be unharmed as long as you deliver the money with no strings attached and as long as the police are not contacted. Are we clear?"

"We're clear," Buck confirmed grudgingly.

The voice laughed, the sound a disgusting warble. "I'm certain you would like very much to kill me right now," he said. "But just think, if I hadn't brought your daughter's existence to your attention, you might never have known about her. Ironic, don't you think?"

The connection severed before Buck could react.

He closed the phone and handed it back to Jenna. It was twelve-forty now.

"We have ten minutes and then we should go. We drop the money and he's going to let Becca go unharmed."

The terror that gripped her once more flashed in her eyes and made his heart wrench painfully.

"Do you believe him? Do you think he'll keep his word?"

She needed him to comfort her, to give her the hope she wanted desperately to cling to.

"I think we don't have a choice either way."

For the first time since the nightmare began, Buck realized something he'd been denying. This could go very, very wrong. Just like Saul said. And there wasn't a damned thing he could do to alter the momentum.

CHAPTER SEVEN

UNCLAIMED BAGGAGE WAS the small town of Scottsboro's secret weapon when it came to drawing in shoppers and tourists. The independent operation had drawn coverage from *Good Morning America* to *The Late Show*. The city's claim to fame. They took lost and unclaimed goods from airlines and sold them at half their original value, or less depending upon condition, and voilà, everyone was happy. People came from all over the country to shop at this famous hot spot.

That was exactly why Buck wouldn't have considered this location as the drop point. The place was always busy.

Maybe that was the idea.

Who could read the mind of a madman?

"This doesn't make sense."

He turned to Jenna and offered a reassuring smile. It wasn't one of his better efforts, but it was the best he could do. "It doesn't, but following his orders is our only option."

She stared up at him, the desperation and fear in

her eyes making him ache deep inside. "You're sure he said you had to go in alone."

Buck nodded. "I know this is difficult, Jen, but we can't deviate."

She looked across the parking lot at the shoppers filing into the large store. "I'll wait here then."

The digital clock on the dash signaled it was time. "I'll be right back."

Buck climbed out of his SUV, briefcase in hand, and headed for the main entrance. He had no idea if he would be stopped by an employee. Would he even be allowed to go into the store carrying a briefcase? Only one way to find out.

He walked in and glanced around. The crowd helped him relax. No one appeared to take any particular note of his arrival or the briefcase in his hand. The upper level was to his right. He moved in that direction, ascended the half-dozen steps that took him to the designated area. On his left was the luggage department. Taking a moment to assess the location, he walked through the racks of luggage. There were backpacks and a number of briefcases. No question, this was the place.

With one final look around, he placed the briefcase he carried on the floor next to another similar one. He straightened and walked away. He wanted to look back just to see if anyone had been watching, but he didn't.

Outside he went straight to his Escalade and slid in behind the steering wheel.

Neither he nor Jenna spoke. What was there to say? They had one option now. Wait for the next call.

"He said we should drive away immediately. Why don't we go back to your place and wait?" The cold had started to creep inside the vehicle.

She nodded. He understood the need for quiet. Speaking would have been too difficult.

They'd held up their end of the deal. They'd given the scum exactly what he asked for. Now they were back to the waiting.

JENNA couldn't sit.

She stood at the window in her living room staring out at nothing in particular.

Buck sat on the sofa behind her. He hadn't said anything else since they'd arrived back at her place. The silence felt so oppressive each breath was a tremendous labor. But talking was out of the question. If she opened her mouth, the sobs would break free. She could feel the urge to wail pressing against her throat.

She'd prayed over and over. Willing it to ring, she held the phone, didn't dare lay it aside. The bastard had the money. Why didn't he call? She pushed the thought away. If she let herself start thinking like that she would break down. She couldn't break down. She had to be strong.

The time crept by, and the agony increased with each minute that passed.

And the call didn't come.

She checked the bars again, made sure she had service even though she knew she did. She'd used her phone from here a million times. She checked the charge just to be sure the battery wasn't low.

And she waited some more.

Nothing.

The misery closed in on her.

The call wasn't coming.

"Jen."

Buck moved up behind her, touched her shoulder. She flinched as much from the sound of his voice as from his touch. They hadn't spoken in more than an hour.

"We need to consider calling the police."

"No." She whipped around to face him. "He said he would kill her if we called the police."

Hadn't Buck been listening?

The way he looked at her, with all that sympathy, she knew what he was thinking. He thought it was over. That she wasn't getting her daughter back.

Well, she wouldn't believe that. No way.

"Darlin', I'm afraid he isn't going to call. The longer we wait the less likely the police will be able to pick up his trail. We've waited an hour. Continuing to play by his rules may be a mistake."

"Don't say that!" she snarled. The pressure on her chest, the tightness in her throat, was suffocating now.

"We have to do something, Jen. We can't just stand around her and pretend this isn't happening."

She couldn't take it any longer. She fell apart. The sobs shook her violently. Her entire body shuddered with the anguish she could no longer suppress.

Buck held her, murmured nonsensical words to her.

She just wanted her little girl back.

Why? Why was he doing this? He had his money.

She didn't know how long she cried, but eventually there were no more tears and the sobs subsided.

When she'd regained control of herself, Buck drew back far enough to look into her eyes. "I want you to wash your face. We're not sitting here waiting any longer. We're going to do something."

She didn't question his intentions. She didn't have the strength. Part of her knew he was right. Waiting any longer would be insane.

In the bathroom she gasped at her reflection. Her eyes were swollen and red, the color a stark contrast to her overly pale skin. She looked like death warmed over. And she didn't care. But presenting a rational appearance to the police could make the difference in how they viewed her case. She had to be strong. She had to be calm and reasonable.

When she had washed her face with cool water and regained as much of her composure as possible, she returned to the living room. Buck was on the phone. Not her cell, she still had it with her.

"We'll be right over." He hung up and settled his gaze on her. "The owner of Unclaimed Baggage has agreed to allow us to view the security surveillance video. There's a camera in each department, including the luggage department. If we find something on the video, the police could use it to nail him."

"We might be able to see him?" Hope welled. If they had him on camera taking the money, at least they had some chance at catching him.

"Maybe." He snagged her hand. "Let's go."

The drive across town had her hopes building. She tried not to let them build too high, but it was no use. She was desperate. If the man was on the tape, he could be identified. Which meant going to the police. But, at this point, she could hardly argue.

The owner met them at the entrance. The store was still fairly crowded. He led the way to the office, explaining as they went, "I viewed the video of the luggage department. Less than a minute after you left the briefcase someone picked it up. I couldn't believe what I saw."

Anticipation seared through Jenna's veins. "Can you see his face?"

The owner nodded. "That's what I found so hard to believe."

Jenna didn't understand. Evidently Buck didn't either since he asked, "What do you mean?"

"The man who picked up your briefcase is a former employee."

Jenna's gaze met Buck's, and his reaction was just as hesitant and restrained as her own. Neither knew whether to be excited at the possible break or to be terrified that this was something far more sinister than an attempt to extort money. Did she or had she ever known anyone employed at Unclaimed Baggage? Did Buck?

They gathered around the monitor in the owner's office and observed as the video was fast-forwarded to the point where Buck left the briefcase as ordered. All other thoughts vanished from Jenna's mind. She watched as Buck walked out of the camera's viewing angle. Several seconds passed, maybe thirty, then a few more before another man entered the camera's field of view. He walked straight to the briefcase as if he'd monitored its arrival. He picked it up and that was when things took a bizarre turn. He stopped, lifted his face toward the camera and stared for a full ten seconds before leaving.

The owner froze that frame. "You see." He pointed at the monitor. "This is Calvin Hastings. He used to work here. He knew where the camera was located. Knew its angle. It's almost as if he looked directly at it on purpose."

Something dark that she couldn't label slithered to life deep inside Jenna. Whatever she had thought when that first call came, she had been wrong. This was far worse than anything she could have imagined. Her heart thudded hard and the sensation of drowning all but overwhelmed her.

"Do you have this man's current address?" Buck asked.

"I've already pulled the information for you." The owner passed a note to Buck. "Look, Hastings is a bit of a bum. Doesn't like to work on a regular basis, but this guy is no criminal. I don't know what this is about, but I can tell you right now something is very, very wrong with this picture." He tapped the screen once more. "Lazy he might be, but the guy isn't stupid."

"Thank you for your assistance, Mr. Olson." Buck shook the man's hand. "You've been extremely helpful."

"I wish there was more I could do," Olson offered.

"Keeping our meeting quiet is all we can ask," Buck reminded.

Olson nodded. "Not to worry. No one will know. I'll put the video in the safe until I hear from you again. In case—" he glanced at Jenna "—you need it for anything else."

"We appreciate that more than you can imagine."

"I remember when you were still driving," Olson went on, delaying their exit. "You were the best. You put NASCAR on the map for me." He glanced at Jenna again. "Listen, I don't mean to get into your business but this sounds like something the police need to handle." His gaze settled on Buck. "Are you sure you're doing the right thing?"

The expression on Buck's face made Jenna's heart plummet to her stomach. He'd been so strong, so certain, but she saw the worry and the fear just then and it scared her to death. If he had started to doubt…she couldn't even think it. She couldn't.

"We're playing by the rules we were given. We don't have a choice. If we don't follow his instructions…well, you get the idea."

"Of course." Olson looked pained. "No one will hear about this from me and no one will see this video without your explicit authorization or a court order."

"Thank you."

Buck ushered Jenna from the office.

The movement awakened that dark, slithering terror again. "What're we going to do now?" For the first time since they made the drop she started to consider that going to the police might be the only thing left to do. The fear spurted in her chest, making her heart flail helplessly. God help her, she was so afraid for her little girl.

"We're going to pay Mr. Hastings a visit." He pushed the exit door open for her. "I'm pretty sure what we saw on that video was an invitation."

Jenna considered the way the man had looked at the camera and she had to agree. "The only question is why."

"That," Buck said as they reached his SUV, "is what we're going to find out." He handed her the address. "Tell me the way."

CALVIN HASTINGS lived on a small, narrow street where shotgun houses still stood as a reminder of days gone by. The exterior's tan color had faded to a dingy off-white. A shutter hung at an unintended angle from the window it flanked, its brown paint peeling to reveal a worn-out shade of green beneath.

An old pickup truck was parked in the drive. Smoke curled up from the chimney, giving every indication that somebody was home.

According to Mr. Olson, Hastings lived alone, so it should be him. Buck shut off the engine.

"I'd like you to stay in the car, Jenna."

"No way. I'm going in."

As much as he'd prefer she stay out here in the safety of the vehicle, he understood how she felt. "All right, but stay behind me as best you can. I don't want you getting hurt. We don't know what to expect in there."

"We know this isn't the man who has my daughter," she countered.

He'd already considered that. A man who went to such lengths to disguise his voice wasn't going to show his face on camera at a former place of employment. The best they could hope for was that Calvin Hastings could provide a lead to the man who had taken Becca.

"Let's see what Mr. Hastings has to say."

Buck led the way to the door. He knocked, three swift raps.

"It's open," a voice called, adding another layer of unease to the situation.

Buck reminded Jenna, "Stay behind me."

When she nodded her understanding, he twisted

the knob and entered the house. Standing on the threshold of the front door he could see straight through the house, all the way to the backdoor, hence the name shotgun house. On some level he was surprised that the owner wasn't already bolting out that backdoor. Mr. Calvin Hastings sat in a chair no more than ten feet from the front door. He made no move to get up and didn't appear to be armed.

"I've been waiting for you."

Armed or not, the man's statement was creepy. "Then you must know why we're here."

Hastings nodded, his expression blank. "He told me to tell you that the game has just begun. The next move is his, he'll call when he's ready."

"Who is he?" Buck demanded more harshly than he'd intended. This guy's cooperation could be essential, so scaring him wouldn't help toward that end.

Hastings shook his head. "I don't know."

Buck took a step in his direction, opting for a little encouragement after all. "How did he contact you?"

Hastings looked at the phone on the table next to the crappy sofa. "He called two days ago. Told me what to do." His gaze settled on Buck's once more. "Told me what he'd do if I didn't follow his instructions to the letter."

"Can you tell me anything about his voice?" Buck pressed, moving yet another step closer.

"It was weird, like something from some futuristic movie."

"So you have no idea who this might be or why he chose you?"

There had to be a reason. A connection. Buck was counting on it.

"He said he knew I got fired from my job and that I deserved better. He said he'd pay me twice what I'd earn in a year there if I did what he said. If I didn't he'd…" The man's throat worked but no more words came.

"He'd what?" Buck was standing right next to his chair now, amping up the intimidation factor. Hastings peered up at him, seemingly unafraid or too stressed to care.

"My mother's in the nursing home over by the hospital. He said if I didn't do what he said, he'd make sure she was tortured before she was suffocated." His eyes locked with Buck's. "She had a stroke. She's aware of everything around her but she can't move or speak." He swallowed hard, the muscles of his throat working frantically. "I wanted to stay with her every minute since he called but he said if I went near the nursing home, if I told anyone, he'd make me wish I hadn't."

"And you had reason to believe he could follow through on this threat?"

The man's bleak gaze connected fully with Buck's once more. "The nursing home called right after he hung up and said they'd found her on the floor in her room." His laugh was dry and fragile. "The nurse thought maybe she'd tried to get up. Thought it might be a good sign. But I knew it was him."

Buck couldn't help feeling sorry for the man, but he had to be firm. He needed more information. "Think, Mr. Hastings, there has to be someone who knows you well enough to be aware of your job trials and your mother's illness."

"That's all I've done for two days." He looked away. "I've asked myself that same question over and over. I can't help you, Mr. Buchanan."

Buck grabbed him by the collar and jerked him to his feet. "How did you know my name?" The fury he'd been holding back blasted through the sympathy, making him want to beat the hell out of this man even if he was a victim, too.

"He told me who to expect!" The fear in his voice, in his eyes, backed up his words. "He told me your name."

"Buck." Jenna tugged at his sleeve. "Don't."

Buck released him. His rage roared in and out of his lungs like fire. He wanted to tear something or someone apart. Maybe this guy was on the up-and-up. Maybe he was a victim, too, but the desperation was closing in on Buck. He needed someone to blame. Needed someone to hold responsible.

"He'll call when he's ready," Hastings repeated. "The only thing you can do is wait."

Buck turned away from the man and urged Jenna toward the door. Fury and determination roiled through him with every step. This had gone far enough.

Outside he assisted Jenna into the passenger seat and then he loaded in behind the wheel. He started the engine, shifted into Reverse and lunged out onto the street.

He wasn't playing this bastard's game any longer.

"Where are we going?"

Jenna's voice was small and tentative as she looked around at the passing landscape in an attempt to determine his destination.

"We're doing what we should have done last night. We're going to the police."

"No!" She twisted in her seat as far as the seat belt would allow. "We can't do that! Not now. You heard what Hastings said. He's going to call. The next move is his."

Buck didn't slow. He was driving straight to the police and reporting this whole crazy scheme. This was exactly what they should have done yesterday. Every minute they wasted was one that gave this crazy bastard more room to yank their chains. He'd pushed until they were in the danger zone. Only a fool pressed his luck when he was in the danger zone. This scumbag was getting away with this and they were letting him by not going to the police.

"Buck, please. We can't!"

He ignored her pleas. She was reacting on emotion. She wasn't thinking clearly. He couldn't say his reasoning was completely free of emotion, but his was a hell of a lot closer to rational than hers and someone had to make the right choice.

"He'll hurt Becca," she cried when he didn't slow down.

"He's not going to let her go, Jen. Don't you see that?" He glanced at her, needed her to understand that this was some sort of sick game they couldn't possibly hope to win.

"Stop the car!" Jenna released her seat belt and reached for the door as if she intended to make a jump for it. "I'm not going with you. If you do this and my daughter dies, I swear I'll…"

He manacled her arm but didn't slow his race toward help. "You're not thinking this through. Someone has to. We're going to the police."

He held on to her as he made the journey across town. He wheeled into the station's parking lot and came to a haphazard stop in one of the slots. He jammed the gearshift into Park with his free hand and cut the engine.

"You listen to me," he urged. "If we don't act fast, it'll be too late and the police won't be able to help us. We have to do this for Becca's sake."

The tears brimmed past her lashes. Her lips trembled, but there was nothing fragile about her words when she spoke. "You're going to get her killed. That's what you're going to do. Damn you, Buck Buchanan. You're supposed to be helping me!"

Her cell phone burst into sound.

Their gazes held for one trauma-filled moment before shifting to the phone clutched in her hand.

Fear and tension hung so heavy in the air a decent breath was impossible.

She checked the screen before meeting Buck's eyes once more. "It's him."

CHAPTER EIGHT

"PUT BUCHANAN ON the line."

Jenna shuddered at the hideous sound of the voice she'd come to identify with sheer terror. "You have the money," she pleaded, her throat clenched with anguish. "Where is my daughter?"

"Put Buchanan on the line or I will hang up."

Her hand shaking, Jenna passed the phone to Buck. She struggled to hold back the sobs quaking in her chest but she wasn't entirely successful as a choking hiccup escaped.

Buck took the cell from her and pressed the button to activate the speaker phone so they could both hear what he had to say. "Buchanan."

"I've left a gift for you."

Jenna's heart jolted in her chest. Please, please let him tell them where Becca was. Please let her be safe. He had his money, why was he doing this? She grappled for a reason when this twisted man clearly knew no reason.

"Selecting the perfect place to leave such an important gift was no easy feat," the garbled voice said.

"Then I realized that the best choice was the final resting place of has-beens. A place where things no longer useful are left to rot. A cemetery of sorts."

A new kind of terror exploded in Jenna's veins. He couldn't mean—

"What do you want?" Buck growled savagely. He'd shut off the speaker phone option and jammed the phone against his ear so she couldn't hear.

Her lungs couldn't draw in enough air. She couldn't think, couldn't wrap her brain around what that final statement meant. *Cemetery?*

Buck listened, his jawline visibly tightening, then he closed the phone and laid it on the console between them. He wouldn't meet Jenna's gaze at first. Oddly, that scared her more than anything the man had said.

"We have to drive back to my place."

She wanted desperately to demand what else he'd been told, but she couldn't bear the possibility that it was worse news.

The idea was too unthinkable. She just couldn't go there. Refused. Facing forward she clasped her ice-cold hands in her lap and stared straight ahead.

Her daughter would be fine. God would not allow this travesty to occur. She had to believe that. They would go back to Buck's house, and then…what?

"I don't understand." She dared to glance at Buck as he pulled out onto the street, leaving the police department behind. She told herself it was the right thing to do. He had said he would hurt Becca if they went to the police. Maybe he was watching and that was why he'd been nastier than before in his most recent call. Maybe they had made him angry. They had to be more careful. "Why are we going back to your house?" Surely the answer to that one question wouldn't be so bad. There had to be some logical explanation.

"In one hour he's going to call and give us a location."

Hope soared past all the fear and misery. "Becca's location?"

Buck exhaled a ragged breath. "I don't know."

That was where she left it. Whether it was something in his voice or that word...*cemetery*...that frightened her back into silence she couldn't say.

They'd go to Buck's home and the call would come and then she would get her daughter back. She refused to believe anything else.

She stared at the highway in front of them, allowed the white line to distract her, hypnotize her. She blanked her mind then, told herself not to think at all. Forty minutes would feel like a lifetime if she let the concept filter past the protective mental walls she had built. So she didn't.

It was the only way to tolerate the horrific pressure swelling in her chest.

Don't think. *Believe.* Just believe.

BUCK PARKED in front of his house. Twenty minutes before the call would come. No point pulling into the garage since they would be leaving again soon. He almost laughed out loud at the thought.

What was happening here?

Everything was out of control.

His entire life he'd been a take-charge kind of guy. When trouble happened, he jumped in and took care of the situation. That was his way. He'd never run into an obstacle he couldn't move, shake or persuade.

This time was different.

This time he felt lost.

He knew. *He knew* this was about him. The goal was to injure him somehow. The notion that this game intended to damage him by hurting an innocent little girl made him want to howl like a wounded animal. Made him want to turn this town and the next upside-down until he found this son of a bitch and made him pay.

Yet there was nothing he could do but wait for the call.

The next move is his.

The reality that he was entirely helpless against this threat left him stunned and somehow vulnerable.

"Let's go inside. I'll make some coffee." He shifted in his seat to look at his passenger. Jenna hadn't spoken since asking the question that had ripped his heart right out of his chest. *Becca's location?*

"I'll just wait out here." She glanced at the cell phone lying on the console. "I want to be ready when he calls."

"Jenna."

"You go ahead," she urged without meeting his gaze. "I'll be fine."

"I'll bring you a cup."

She didn't respond to the offer. He hated to leave her out here like this but there was something he had to do. He'd thought long and hard on the drive back here. It was true that his hands were, for all intents and purposes, tied. But there was one small thing he could set in motion, and it might not help but it couldn't possibly hurt.

He opened the door and got out, but hesitated before closing it. Staring straight ahead, she maintained that silent vigil. It didn't take much imagination to estimate what was going through her head. They had turned over the money as instructed and still she didn't have her little girl back. She would consider what they could possibly have done wrong or differently.

This had to be pure torment. A mother's worst nightmare.

Anything he could do would be better than nothing.

He closed the door with a soft thud and headed inside. After unlocking the front door and entering the code to deactivate the alarm, he went directly to the kitchen. Once the coffee was brewing, he fished out his own cell phone and made a call to George Farley.

"George, I need your help."

Buck didn't have a lot of enemies. Sure he'd made a few, but after twenty years in the high-octane sport of stock car racing, keeping it down to a few was a damned fine accomplishment.

But he knew of at least three he'd made in over two decades of pushing to win. Buddy Reed, the driver he'd given the boot when he brought Rush Jackson on board; Addison Lombardo, a team owner he'd reported a decade ago for attempting to utilize illegal technology that would have endangered his driver as well as anyone else on the track with him; and, of course, there was Tom McElroy.

George was ready and willing to do whatever he could. And, thankfully, he didn't ask any unnecessary questions. "I know you're packing up for Daytona, but I want you to find out what McElroy is up to. You could look up Lombardo, but I think that would be a waste of time. The man was in a wheelchair and half dead the last I heard. If he was going to give me any grief, he'd have done it years ago. Still, this thing has something to do with me and someone I've crossed." It pained Buck to say it but he was more sure than he wanted to be. "I want to know where McElroy is and what he's doing with his time. Get Lori and Saul and anybody else you need to help you, but let's keep it quiet. If McElroy's involved, we don't want him getting wind that we're poking around. He's probably still madder than hell that I fired him." Buck shook his head. "I just can't see him doing something like this but I can't be sure. Whoever this bastard is, he's watching every move we make."

Buck ended the call with complete confidence that his people would find some answers for him. That would allow him to focus on this twisted game. In his estimation, that was part of the point. Keep him and Jenna distracted so they couldn't actually do anything useful in an effort to find Becca.

Not to mention that once he knew his opponent, he'd have a better handle on what to expect and how to anticipate his moves.

Buck was reasonably sure Buddy Reed had moved on. He'd gotten himself hooked up with another team. He hadn't achieved the star status he'd hoped for but if there were any hard feelings still lingering between them, Buck hadn't heard about it. As big as NASCAR was, it could still be a small world. He would have heard if Buddy still held a grudge. But maybe not.

The dirty business with Tom McElroy, on the other hand, was still fresh. His situation ended with an understanding that he was no longer welcome in NASCAR. That was a major blow, far more shattering than Buck firing him.

Fury came to a boil in Buck's gut. He'd known Tom since grade school. The idea that he could betray the people he worked with every day—people he called friends—was despicable.

But this…this went way beyond mere despicable. If McElroy had anything to do with this little girl's disappearance, there wouldn't be any place on this planet that he could hide. That was one score Buck would settle outside the law.

That this kidnapping came only a couple months after McElroy's betrayal had Buck leaning in that direction. Besides, McElroy had been there when Jenna left. He would have more likely come to the conclusion that Becca was Buck's daughter.

This had to be his doing.

Buck shook his head. If McElroy could tinker with a few pictures that found their way to major newspapers to make Buck's driver look bad and risk the loss of sponsors why not kidnap a child? How could the man do something like that?

Had he gone completely crazy?

McElroy had to be found.

The smell of coffee had permeated the kitchen while Buck was lost in thought. He searched through the cupboards until he found a couple of travel mugs. With both topped off he clicked off the coffeemaker and wasted no time getting back outside to Jenna. They still had four or five minutes before the call was scheduled to come. He left the coffee on a window ledge long enough to activate the alarm and lock the door.

Jenna sat staring out the windshield, same as he'd left her. He wished there was something he could do to reassure her, but there was nothing. Nothing outside finding her daughter safe and sound was going to heal the hurt ripping her apart even as he watched.

He'd blocked the whole concept that her daughter

was his daughter as well. He couldn't deal with this dirtbag and his calls if he let himself focus on the idea that his child…his only child…was in danger.

He needed to tell Reba. His sister would be furious that she'd been left out of this loop. But at the moment there was no margin for error. The fewer people who knew, the better. He would get word to her as soon as it was safe to do so.

With the handles of both coffee mugs clutched in one hand, he opened the driver's side door of his SUV. He placed both mugs in the cupholders on the console before settling into the driver's seat.

When Jenna still didn't glance his way or speak, he said, "I didn't think to ask if you needed to go inside for anything. I can give you the key if you'd like. The security code's easy, it's a double eighty-six. We still have a couple minutes if you need anything."

"I don't need to go in. I don't need anything."

"Coffee's good," he assured. He wasn't much of a cook but he could make a hell of a cup of coffee. He took a sip and moaned his satisfaction to punctuate his comment.

She didn't touch hers.

When the cell phone heralded its tune, she turned her head to stare down at it a moment before she reached to pick it up. That was when Buck realized just how much trouble they were in here. She was a nurse but she didn't recognize the symptoms. He damn sure did, at least he did now. She was getting shocky on him. That explained the extended silence, the inability to leave the vehicle, the steady unblinking gaze. She needed the coffee.

"Hello."

Her voice was small and flat. The sound wrenched his chest.

"Yes."

She swiveled in Buck's direction and held the phone out to him. "He'll only talk to you."

He took the phone but he didn't let go of her hand. He pressed her hand down to the mug. When her gaze bumped into his he gave her a look that urged her to drink. Her fingers wrapped around the warm mug and he lifted the phone to his ear.

"Buchanan."

"Beyond your city limits there's a giant graveyard where the past lies dying. In that place of rusting metal and broken glass you'll find the gift I've left you. But you must hurry. There's a cold front moving in. With the sky so clear the temperatures are expected to drop well below freezing tonight."

Anger and desperation rocketed inside Buck. "How can you tell me to hurry when I'm not even sure where I'm going?" The ridiculously riddle-like description he'd given whirled in his head.

"I'm certain you'll figure it out, Buck. You're a legend, after all." Laughter, garbled and gnarled, echoed across the connection. "Hurry now, don't be late. Blood cools swiftly when it's this cold."

The connection dropped off.

Jenna held the mug in both hands, as if the warmth it offered was somehow sustaining her. "Where is she?" The watery expression combined with the fragile words damaged him on a level that no other tragedy, no other pain, had ever touched.

He held up a hand for her to wait. He had to think. Couldn't let his emotions get too strong a hold on him. A giant graveyard beyond the city limits. Rusting metal, shattered glass.

A salvage yard—junkyard some would call it— where automobiles, wrecked or simply no longer in working condition were sold off as spare parts or just left to disintegrate…to rot.

There were several in Madison County but only one that came immediately to mind. Trader's Salvage Yard. The place was huge and it claimed a few acres just north of the city limits, which meant a thirty-minute trip and only a couple of hours of daylight left.

How the hell were they supposed to cover a place that size in an hour or two?

He would need help.

He would need his team.

JENNA LEANED FORWARD in her seat when Buck pulled into the parking area of a junkyard. The place looked deserted and ominous. The line of rusting junkers and newer-looking cars and trucks that had been crashed appeared to roll out for acres. The gravel parking area flanking the trailer-turned-office was empty and the office was dark.

Definitely deserted.

"This is where he said to come?"

This didn't make sense. She surveyed the vast field of damaged vehicles. Surely her daughter wasn't here.

The thought had no more formed in her head than another car rolled into the parking lot.

Then another after that.

Disbelief and fear commingled, sending Jenna's heart into a panic.

"What did you do, Buck?"

He met her gaze, his own implacable. "We have less than two hours of daylight left. We needed help, Jenna. We can't do this alone."

Her breath stalled in her lungs as she surveyed the acres of oxidizing and damaged metal once more. There were so many places to hide. "Oh, God."

A towering chain-link fence raced along the boundary of the property on all sides for as far as she could see. The side that ran parallel with the road was obscured with green webbing in an effort to camouflage the ugliness of what lay behind. But here, she could see clearly beyond the massive drive-thru gate that towered next to the office, heavy chains holding it closed. How would they even get in there?

She was out of the vehicle and headed for the gate

before the command fully synapsed in her brain. She had to get to her daughter.

Could she climb the gate? She stared upward, and estimated the height at ten or maybe twelve feet. She had to try.

"Hold up, Jenna."

George Farley strode toward her, a large tool in his right hand. She frowned. A tool similar to the long-handled pruning shears she had at home. The kind used for clipping small tree limbs. No, she decided as he drew closer. Not shears…bolt cutters.

With just two quick snaps the chain fell away. A young man she recognized as Buck's driver, Rush Jackson, helped Farley pull the gate open just far enough to slip through.

Buck waited for her to go ahead of him. She threaded easily through the opening. Buck followed. Then Lori Houser and Charlene Talley. The team members Buck had called in as backup were well-prepared, all wore jeans and sweat shirts, gloves and hiking boots.

Lori passed Jenna a pair of gloves. "You might need these." She offered a pair to Buck as well.

Rush provided flashlights for everyone. "We may run out of daylight," he commented with a brief smile at Jenna. "This'll help."

George had pushed the gate back to its closed position and hung the chain so that it looked as if it were still locked. If the owner drove by he would know something was up. She supposed the effect was for anyone else who might notice the vehicles parked in the lot after hours.

Buck called out names and search directions. "Watch where you poke your heads and your hands. We could run into hibernating snakes, skunks, who knows what."

That was when she heard the growl.

Jenna swiveled right and her gaze locked with the biggest, meanest dog she'd ever laid eyes on.

"Come on, boy." George squatted a few yards from where the dog hovered in the attack position. The animal's teeth were bared. The hair on his back stood on end. "How about some dinner, fella?"

Jenna watched in amazement as George un-wrapped a hamburger from a local fast food restau-rant and offered the dog the cooked patty. These people really had thought of everything.

It took maybe a minute and a half, during which time nobody moved, but George lured the animal to him. After he'd fed the scrappy-looking dog a couple of burgers, patted him and scratched him behind the ears, he had a friend for life. George rose up to a standing position. "Come on, boy, let's go see what we can find." He headed off in the direction Buck had given him, the dog right on his heels.

Buck wrapped his fingers around her arm and urged her forward. "Let's get started."

Jenna wanted to cry. She knew these people hated

her and yet here they were trying to help her find her daughter. She thanked God for that blessing. Then she cleared her mind and focused on searching the damaged vehicles.

Buck had been right. Before they were anywhere near finished, the bleak afternoon had darkened into night. With the sky clear and millions of stars sprinkled across its darkness, it was cold…colder than the night before.

She was numb with fear or the cold or both. They'd called Becca's name a thousand times. Jenna had cried when her voice was too hoarse to call out anymore. But she couldn't stop searching. If it took all night, she had to keep looking. Becca would be scared to death, tied up as she surely was, and maybe gagged in this awful place.

The sound of running footsteps had Buck shifting the beam of light to the darkness behind them. Jenna's attention followed the beam. Rush Jackson skidded to a stop in the light's path, held his hand up to protect his eyes.

"Buck, there's something over here you need to see."

"Is it—?" Buck didn't finish his question.

Maybe it was the sick-with-dread expression on Jackson's face or maybe some sixth sense that warned him this was bad. Jenna felt paralyzed. If she didn't move, she wouldn't have to see. If she didn't see, she wouldn't have to believe.

They'd found something.

CHAPTER NINE

THE CAR WASN'T ONE she readily recognized the make of. Something blue or black. Four doors. The front had been smashed all the way into the driver's seat in a crash that hadn't taken place anytime recently.

It sat next to an old green truck like one her daddy used to own when she'd been a kid. The truck had been scavenged for its left fender and the hood.

Lori, Charlene and George waited by the car. Rush and Buck were shining their flashlights into the backseat as they peered through the open window.

Jenna stood a few steps back. She didn't want to see. She just wanted this over. She wanted to go home and curl up in her bed with one of her daughter's stuffed animals.

Then she could go to sleep and forget about this day.

"God Almighty."

The misery in Buck's voice tugged her attention back to him. A little burst of adrenaline detonated in her chest. She ignored it, refused to be baited to action.

This was not happening.

She would not believe it.

"You want me to climb in there and see what we've got?" Rush asked quietly. "We tried opening the door but it won't budge."

"Hold the light," Buck instructed. "I'll do it."

Reality broadsided Jenna in that instant. The impact came with such force that it took her breath.

She had to know.

She propelled herself forward, maneuvered between Buck and Rush. Her gaze landed on the object in the dilapidated backseat of the brutalized vehicle.

The long black object was at first unfamiliar to her.

Recognition hit in a heart-stopping instant.

Body bag.

A keening sound rose up in the air and it wasn't until Buck grabbed her and hauled her away from the vehicle that she realized it had come from her.

"Nooooo!" she cried, the anguish unbearable, suffocating.

"It might not be her, Jen. Listen to me!"

She tried to focus on his face, on his words, but the world was spinning. "No," she mewled.

The metal-on-metal slide of a zipper being lowered shattered the thick silence.

Jen's instincts sharpened and her attention jerked back to the car. She wrenched free of Buck's hold and ran to the open window, her heart ramming against her sternum with enough force to rupture the organ.

Inside the car, Rush's hands shook as he parted the sides of the somber bag.

Jen blinked, fought the black that threatened her consciousness. Told herself to focus.

Green…splotches of red.

"That son of a bitch," Buck snapped.

Money. The body bag contained money.

The money was splattered with red splotches… blood.

Jenna went ice cold all over again.

Before she could stop herself, she started scrambling through the window.

"Wait, Jen!" Buck hauled her away from the vehicle. "Don't touch anything else, Rush."

"Let me go!" She yanked at his hold but this time he wasn't letting her loose. "I need to see."

"Ma'am," Rush said as he threaded his way out the window, "there's nothing in there but piles of money and what looks like blood or red paint splattered on some of the bills. I promise that's all there is."

Jen wilted in Buck's arms. Oh, God, oh, God. What did this mean? Where was her baby?

"Call Sheriff Sykes," Buck said. "We've done all we can do."

Rush had left his flashlight in the car. The glow provided enough light for Jenna even from where she stood to see the spots of red on the money.

Please, God, don't let it be blood.

She suddenly wondered why she kept bothering to pray. So far no one appeared to be listening.

A part of her ceased to exist at that moment.

She thought of all the crime dramas she'd seen where they talked about the importance of the first forty-eight hours after someone went missing. Well, she'd let this bastard talk her into letting a good portion of that first forty-eight go by without contacting the police. Now the chances of them finding her daughter would be extremely slim.

Her mistake may have cost her daughter's life.

BUCK KEPT JENNA close to him as the sheriff called in his forensics technicians and the dogs. Sheriff Sykes had allowed Charlene and Rush to go home after giving their statements. George and Lori had refused to leave. Lori suggested repeatedly that Buck permit her to take Jenna home, but he didn't want her out of his sight.

The bands on the money marked it as having come from his bank. If he had his guess it was the same money he'd dropped off in the briefcase just a few hours ago.

What kind of game was this lunatic playing?

While the technicians did their job, and the dogs were walked around the property, Sheriff Sykes herded Buck and Jenna into his personal vehicle.

"Buck, I need you and Ms. Williams to start at the beginning and tell me everything that's happened."

The truck that pulled into the parking lot just then bore the Trader's logo. The owner, Buck surmised. Sykes had probably called him since it was his property, and also to get some idea of who might have had access to the property this afternoon. It was pretty hard not to notice a guy carrying a body bag. Like Buck, Sykes had deduced that the perpetrator executed his dirty business after the salvage yard closed. On Saturdays closing time was noon.

Funny how that coincided with the call he and Jenna had received.

"Ms. Williams, I know this is difficult, but I need you to go over the events of Friday evening with me. Take your time, we don't want to skip anything. The slightest thing might turn out to be significant."

Buck listened as she repeated in horrifying detail the way she'd worked late because of the accident and then the slow realization that her daughter was not with friends. Listening to her repeat that first call stoked his rage. When he got his hands on the man behind this, he would make him wish he'd never been born.

When Jenna had completed her statement, Sykes turned to Buck. "Why don't you start with Ms. Williams's arrival at your home on Friday night?"

By the time Sykes had finished with his questions the forensics techs had completed their work. Another deputy had questioned the salvage yard owner and they were all free to go. Since the kidnapper was using Becca's cell phone, trying to track the number would be pointless. He intended to contact the FBI regarding an attempted trace on the location of the cell phone. But that would take time and luck.

To track the location of the phone, it had to be turned on and, preferably, in use.

They stood by the open gate leading into the salvage yard. Buck knew he should be freezing but the only thing he felt was drained and defeated. He was certain Jenna felt the same way.

"Ma'am," Sykes said to Jenna, "as soon as we have a confirmation on the blood type we'll let you know."

DNA analysis would take far longer, but at least determining the blood type would tell them if there was a chance it was Becca's blood.

Jenna managed a jerky nod. "Thank you."

"I'm going to authorize surveillance on your home," he said to Buck. "And get clearance to monitor your calls. Yours too, ma'am. Whoever this guy is," he added, "he's planned this for a while. He's got it bad for you, Buck. The idea that he didn't even keep your money, tells me it isn't about financial gain. It's about some kind of revenge. If I were you, I'd be watching my back. This guy is out for blood."

Jenna shuddered. Buck tightened his arm around her shoulder. "We'll be careful, Sheriff."

Sykes looked a little uncomfortable with what he was about to say but he didn't let that stop him. "I checked and you've got a handgun registered."

Buck nodded. "Yeah, 9 mm Ruger."

Sykes glanced around to make sure no one was close. "I'm not telling you to shoot anyone, but I'd keep that weapon handy until this is over. A man needs to be able to defend himself from a threat like this."

As much as Buck disliked the idea of using a weapon, the purpose of having one was for times like this. There was no way to gauge the severity of this threat with any accuracy. By what he knew already, whoever was playing this nasty game meant business. No way could this end well.

"Ma'am," he addressed Jenna again, "I can coordinate surveillance of your home through Scottsboro's department but I would highly discourage you from going home alone. You need someone with you at all times until this is over."

"She won't be going anywhere alone," Buck stated flatly.

Buck hadn't told Sykes the connection between them since he wasn't sure if Jenna wanted to do that. She hadn't mentioned that Buck was her daughter's father so he had to assume she didn't want it brought up. That was fine by him. For now. But Sykes was no fool. He would conclude that Buck was involved for reasons beyond friendship. Maybe he'd put two and two together. Eventually.

Shouting deep in the cemetery of automobiles jerked Jenna's, as well as everyone else's, attention in that direction.

One of the deputies double-timed it over to where she, Buck and Sykes stood by the gate. That the deputy glanced at her before he spoke had dread congealing in her stomach. "Sheriff, there's something over here you need to see."

Jenna felt her body go rigid. Not again. She didn't want there to be more. As long as there was no body she could pretend it wasn't real. She could believe her daughter was still safe and that she would get her back.

Sykes followed his deputy. Jenna and Buck trailed after them. She didn't hurry and Buck didn't seem to, either. She just couldn't take any more of the agony.

But what if they'd found her daughter? She could be alive. She would certainly be restrained, maybe gagged. Jenna had considered that before.

She started to walk faster. Had to catch up.

This could be good news. It didn't have to be bad.

This could mean it was over. Maybe this sick scumbag only wanted to put Buck through a little agony. Maybe he didn't really want to hurt a child.

Her chest ached and tears burned in her eyes by the time she reached the location where three deputies and one forensics tech stood near a pickup truck.

As she moved closer, one of the men flashed his light under the truck. Her heart halted midbeat.

Navy…lump of clothes or a…bag.

"Pull it out from under there," Sykes said as he crouched for a closer look.

A gloved hand reached beneath the truck and dragged out the item.

Gym bag.

Becca's soccer bag!

Buck had to physically restrain Jenna from making a dive for the bag. She wanted to touch it.

"That's Becca's soccer bag," she fairly shouted. "She had it with her when…" The rest of the words died in her throat.

After pulling on a pair of latex gloves the technician handed him, Sykes opened the bag. "Don't touch anything," he said to Jenna, "just take a look and tell me if you can identify what you see."

She crouched near the bag. The urge to touch it, to feel the item she knew for certain her daughter had been holding when this awful man took her, was nearly overwhelming. Her pink *Girls Rule* T-shirt lay on top of the wad of clothes in the bag. A portion of blue denim was visible and part of a sneaker. All her daughter's.

Jenna nodded. "Those are the clothes she wore to school on Friday."

"Would she have been wearing these when she was abducted?"

"No." Becca never bothered to change back into her school clothes after soccer practice. She just came home wearing her soccer clothes, sans the cleats, and hit the shower. "She would have been wearing her soccer clothes. Navy shorts and a white tee."

If her sneakers were still in this bag that meant she hadn't gotten the chance to change out of her cleats. An ache pierced Jenna, stabbed at her heart. She wanted desperately to touch her daughter's clothes, to inhale her precious scent. But there could be important evidence on the bag. So she kept her arms wrapped around her middle to resist the need to reach out.

"We'll have to take this into evidence," Sykes explained gently.

She managed an up-and-down motion of her head.

Buck ushered her to her feet. "Let's move out of their way, Jen, so these gentlemen can do their job."

Jenna walked back to the parking area with him. She didn't look back. Couldn't bear to see them taking her daughter's bag away.

Why couldn't this bastard have taken her instead? Why did it have to be her daughter?

Fury burned through the softer emotions, making her rigid with rage. She hoped he roasted in hell for what he'd done. She closed her eyes, leaned heavily against Buck, and pushed away the images and thoughts that tried to intrude. She didn't want to think.

Buck opened the passenger side door of his SUV and helped her into the seat. She collapsed against the leather, a dozen emotions seeming to crowd in on her at once.

"Buck!"

Jenna opened her eyes, afraid of what they had found now. Sykes hustled over to where Buck waited, one hand on the door ready to close her off from this evolving horror.

"We pulled this letter out of the girl's gym bag."

Sykes held up a plastic evidence bag. A single wrinkled page was inside.

Buck read the letter, his face going stony.

Jenna turned in her seat and reached for the plastic bag. Her blood felt as if it had all drained to her feet and then poured out on the ground. Her brain felt completely out of sync with her body.

The white page was marred by a single line of handwritten text.

There are some things that money cannot buy.

He'd given the money back. Because it wasn't enough. Whatever wrong this man thought Buck had committed, he wasn't going to accept money as reparation. He wanted something more. Something bigger and far more valuable.

He wanted a life. The realization settled in her chest, penetrated the deepest layers of her thoughts. She knew it with complete certainty.

"We're going to finish up here," Sykes explained as he reclaimed the evidence bag containing the letter. "I'd feel a whole lot better if you two went straight to your place, Buck, and stayed put until we have a handle on what this maniac wants. I'm guessing by this note that he's not finished yet."

"You can reach me on my cell," Buck told him. "We won't make a move without keeping you informed."

"I hope you mean that," Sykes countered. "It's going to take everything we've got to beat this guy. Anything you hold back could be crucial."

"Thank you for everything," Buck said. "I've got to get Jenna out of here."

Jenna faced forward once more and Buck closed her door. He rounded the hood and loaded in behind the steering wheel. She couldn't remember ever having been this tired. Not even after a series of double shifts.

She needed to lie down. To sleep. But she was scared to death of the dreams sleep would bring.

She had failed.

Her daughter was out there somewhere....

And Jenna had no idea what to do next.

CHAPTER TEN

BUCK DIVIDED his attention between the road and Jenna. She was hanging on by a thread. She needed some serious sleep, and food would be good. Whatever tomorrow brought she would need all her strength to get through it. He toyed with the idea of calling his personal physician to see about a sedative for her but he was fairly certain she wouldn't go along with that idea.

Rest and food would just have to do. At least for now.

Sheriff Sykes had agreed to call the moment they had the analysis on the blood samples from the body bag. Pain sliced deep. He hoped like hell the blood wouldn't be a match to Becca's type. He just wasn't sure Jenna could take that kind of news. He wasn't even sure he could take it.

As he turned into his driveway he noticed the cruiser stationed in the street at the curb. He was glad for that. This whole mess had taken a jarring turn for the worst. God only knew what would happen next.

This time he opted to park in the garage. Using the

remote clipped onto the visor of his SUV, he deactivated the garage quadrant of the security system and sent the overhead door into the up position. Once he'd parked and shut off the engine, he secured the door and reactivated the system. He wasn't taking any risks tonight.

He turned to Jenna, who sat quietly staring at nothing at all. She'd done a lot of that today. He had to find a way to get her talking again. He couldn't let her withdraw into herself like this.

"You hanging in there?" He wasn't about to ask her if she was okay. She wasn't okay. He'd be a fool to even ask that question.

She took a big, ragged breath. "I'm trying." Her gaze met his, and the sorrow in the gorgeous eyes was almost his undoing. "I have to keep believing that she's coming home." Tears welled. "Can you understand that?"

"I sure can." He placed his hand over hers. She was freezing. He wanted to take her in his arms and hold her until she felt warm and safe again. "I won't give up until we find her."

She stared at his hand for a long moment before meeting his eyes once more. "Thank you, Buck. I don't know how I would have gotten through this without you."

There was a lot more he wanted to say but just then the right words deserted him. It was a hell of a thing. He'd made his mark in the history of NASCAR with his ability to drive well and charm fans. He'd never once found himself at a loss for words. But right now he felt terrified of making a mistake, of somehow saying or doing the wrong thing.

He got out and went around to her side of the vehicle. She'd already opened the door and climbed out. She swayed a little and he offered a hand in support.

"I'm okay, really."

He was crowding her. Time to back off a little. He unlocked the door that led into the kitchen and went through the steps with the security system, careful to reset it once the door was shut and locked. He didn't want any more surprises.

"How about I see what I can throw together. Some good hot soup or chili?" He was pretty sure he still had some of Reba's homemade chili in the freezer. His sister's cooking could take the edge off the worst day.

Jenna's hand fluttered ineffectually. "You go ahead. I'll have something later."

Well, at least it wasn't an outright no. Once he had the concoction warming up maybe the smell would arouse her appetite. He rummaged around in the freezer until he found the plastic container marked *chili*.

After popping it into the microwave to defrost, he decided another pot of coffee was in order. He had some thinking to do and he wanted to touch base with George to see if he'd come up with anything on McElroy. This evening's crisis had kept him from asking what George had found, if anything.

The Westminster chimes of his front doorbell burst into a minisymphony. A frown furrowed its way across his brow. Had Sykes gotten the analysis back already? He could have called. No need for him to come by.

Unless his men had discovered something new at the salvage yard.

A nudge of fear had adrenaline soaring through his body as he made his way to the entryhall. Jenna had turned and was coming back down the stairs, her cell phone still clutched in her hand. One look at her face and he recognized that she, too, was anticipating news on the analysis.

His frown deepened as he checked the security peephole. He turned off the security, then unlocked and opened the door. "What's going on, Lori?"

That his PR rep would show up at his house after this evening's harrowing events felt wrong somehow. It wasn't impossible that she'd heard some news she wanted to pass along. She had all the right connections. If she had learned something relevant she'd want to pass it along in person.

Beyond her shoulder he got a glimpse of George and Saul arriving in their respective vehicles. Now he was really worried.

"Take a look." Lori gestured to the street beyond Buck's expansive front yard.

Several vans sporting satellite dishes and television channel logos had gathered on the street. The officers doing the surveillance had evidently called for back-up since another police cruiser had arrived and was keeping the vultures at bay.

This was unbelievable. He'd been home less than twenty minutes. How could they have moved into position so quickly? Evidently they'd been watching for him to return.

"My contact at the sheriff's department tipped me off when they got the call for backup." Lori came on in. "We were just a few minutes away, grabbing a late dinner."

Buck waited at the door until George and Saul had gotten inside as well.

"I heard they're already on most of the local channels," Lori told him, her tone grim.

Stunned, Buck glanced toward the stairs but Jenna had already turned her back and started up again. He was glad. She didn't need to see or hear any of this. He followed Lori and the others into the great room. Lori grabbed the remote and turned on the big screen.

The ABC affiliate was the first channel she selected. Though the regular programming hadn't been interrupted, the crawler across the bottom of the screen touted breaking news regarding a missing young girl, speculated to be the daughter of Buck Buchanan.

"How the hell did they get that information?" he demanded.

"Outside those of us in this room, and Rush and Charlene, no one else knew, right?" Lori added,

"Except, of course, Jenna and the man who kidnapped her daughter."

Lori flipped to channel after channel and the scene was the same. Two channels were actually showing a live feed from the street outside his home.

"Oh, man!" he muttered.

"Buck, this is exactly what I was afraid of. The negative publicity is going to be immeasurable. Within twenty-four hours they'll start using terms like *illegitimate* and *love child*. It's not going to be pretty. I don't even want to think what the gossip rags are going to do with this."

"We'll deal with whatever they throw our way." He stood his ground. He wasn't afraid of a little bad publicity. This was about him and the past, the long-ago past. In his opinion, there wasn't any aspect of this story that could hurt the team.

Lori looked to George, evidently for backup.

"One of our sponsors called Lori as soon as the story broke. He's concerned that the whole idea of a child you didn't know about tarnishes your image, makes his company look bad for supporting you."

Anger stirred but Buck tamped it down. The sponsors had a right to voice their opinion even when it was wrong. "This is the twenty-first century, boys and girls, the nuclear family is no longer a scene from an episode of *Leave it to Beaver*."

"I agree," Lori piped up. "But the facts will be vastly distorted. You know that. There will be speculation that you tried to hide the child. That you failed to pay child support. That you didn't want a family. You're a forty-year-old single man who has never been married. Elements of the media will jump at the chance to make NASCAR look bad. They'll call you a throwback to the good old days when the thinking was that every driver and team owner was a beer-guzzling, lady's man who shirked his everyday re-sponsibilities to drive fast cars. This could hurt the team when it's so close to Daytona."

Buck understood that Lori's every point offered some validity, but he had bigger problems to deal with just now. What the media did with this story wasn't at the top of his list.

"We all know the media is going to do what they will," he admitted. "We'll just have to deal with it as it happens."

Another of those glances bounced between his crew chief and his PR rep, and this time even his attorney was included.

"What is it the three of you have on your minds?" Buck could sure use that coffee about now. As much as he'd like one, having a good stiff drink was out of the question. He had to be prepared to act if and when another call came.

It would come. It had to.

"We believe," Saul offered, finally breaking his silence, "that it would be in your best interest to make a statement, Buck. Lay the facts out in an attempt to offset some of the speculation. Give the media something real to run with. And maybe they can help get Becca back."

That didn't sound like an entirely bad idea.

"I can see the value in that route. Do you have a strategy?"

Lori shifted, her uneasiness showing. He had worked with Lori for many, many years and he'd never once known her to hold back. She generally came out with whatever she had to say with no care as to what anyone else thought. Except when dealing with the media or sponsors, of course. Then she was the epitome of discretion and savvy, the perfect balance of charm and persuasion.

"To alleviate the sponsor's concerns and to cast a better light on the situation," she began, "I would advise you to tell the truth. Inform the media that you had no idea your daughter existed until twenty-four hours ago. That you were shocked at being left out of her life for all these years and that you intend to take whatever action necessary to make that right once this terrifying business is over."

Buck let her advice penetrate the emotional layers that immediately wanted to challenge her suggestion. He depended upon her to stay on top of what the people, the fans and sponsors, wanted and expected. He trusted her judgment. But this time was different.

"So you want me to make Jenna the bad guy?"

he said for clarification purposes. "Lay all the blame at her feet?"

Saul inclined his head. "Isn't that where it belongs? What Lori is suggesting is the truth. Your fans and sponsors expect you to be on the up-and-up, Buck. Lying or avoiding the facts to protect someone who, frankly, doesn't deserve protecting in this particular part of the equation, would be bad form any way you look at it."

Bad form. God forbid he was ever accused of bad form.

Still, Buck put forth a valiant effort to hang onto his temper, to listen and consider before reacting.

"Look," Lori said, "this isn't fair. Your personal life, especially right now, shouldn't be on display. This is a very painful time. The child you believe is your daughter is missing. You deserve your privacy." She exhaled a heavy breath and braced her hands on her hips. "But the fact of the matter is you don't get that leisure when you're a celebrity. Being at the top comes with a price, Buck, you know that."

Right again. Frankly, he couldn't reasonably argue anything Lori or Saul said.

"This close to Daytona," George spoke up, "we can't have sponsors getting nervous. This isn't my place, Buck, but as your friend I'm telling you that I agree with Lori and Saul. You need to make that statement. You need to put the truth out there in the open."

"Be the underdog," Lori said, running with what

George had started. "Play up the part of the victim. Jenna walked out on you thirteen years ago. She kept your daughter from you all these years. Only when she was in trouble did she come back into your life. Your fans will love you all the more for it."

There it was. The bottom line.

He wanted to be furious with Lori. But this was her job. George and Saul were only looking out for Buck's interests, as well as the team's. He understood all that. But he was still furious.

These loyal people whom he cared a great deal for and whose opinions he greatly respected, deserved an explanation for why he was about to nix their suggestions.

"Yesterday afternoon a twelve-year-old girl was taken from her school yard by a madman," he began. "I can't even bring myself to consider what kind of atrocities she may have suffered at his hands." His pulse pounded at even the thought. "During the hours since, this evil, twisted bastard has led Jenna and me on a wild-goose chase. He has tortured Jenna and made me question all that I've ever believed in. And now, we don't even know if that little girl is still alive." He looked from one speechless member of his team to the other. "Pardon me if I don't give a damn right now what people think. There is a bigger issue at stake here. Saving that child's life." He thumped his chest. "My *daughter's* life."

Silence reigned for about five seconds and then Lori spoke up again. "I know you're hurting, Buck." She flung her arms outward in frustration. "Hell, Jenna has to be losing her mind. And don't you dare suggest that I don't care about that little girl," she challenged, her finger pointed accusingly at him. "I've got kids of my own, dammit. But this—" she planted her hands back on her hips "—this is my job. You pay me to keep you and the team out of trouble with the media and the sponsors. Let me do my job, Buck. You're not thinking rationally right now. Who in your position would be? That's why you've got me and Saul and George here."

"She's right, Buck," Saul urged. "We're only trying to help. When the dust settles from all this, we still have to go on. The season will start whether we're prepared or not. Shall we do our jobs or do we flounder helplessly at the hands of this madman as you so aptly dubbed him?"

George said nothing now. He stared at the floor. Buck was reasonably sure he wasn't as onboard with this whole idea as the other two.

But they were right. This was the job he paid them to do. Protect the team.

"*I'll* make the statement."

At the sound of her voice, Buck whipped around to find Jenna standing in the doorway. God Almighty, she hadn't needed to hear all this. Her face was so pale, her eyes underscored by the dark fear that haunted her heart. He did not want this business to add to her already heavy burden.

"That isn't necessary," he argued. "We'll—"

"That's a brilliant idea," Lori interrupted. She moved toward Jenna. "You give the media the truth and that'll take the heat off Buck."

Jenna nodded. "Since you're the expert," she went on, a bitter edge in her voice, "you draft up a statement and I'll read it to whomever necessary."

"No," Buck objected, his tone nonnegotiable. "We're not giving any statement. This is a private matter. I will not put Jenna through this."

"Buck, you're being unreasonable," Lori protested. "If Jenna wants to make the statement, let her."

Jenna laughed. There wasn't an iota of amusement in the dry, aching sound. "Don't mistake my offer for something I want to do," she said pointedly, her derision clearly directed at Lori. "This has nothing to do with helping you or the team. I got Buck into this mess, I'll make it right. But it won't have a damned thing to do with any of you or your beloved team image."

Lori folded her arms over her chest, fury lashed across her usually composed expression. "Oh, yeah, that's right. You never did care for what we do. How could I have forgotten?"

"That's enough." Buck's jaw clenched to hold back the rage that would only make him say more than was necessary. He'd learned long ago that you couldn't take back the things you said. No amount of apologizing would ever really make up for a damaging statement even when spoken in the heat of the moment.

Lori shook her head. Her frustration settled on Buck. "You know I'm telling the truth."

"Don't," Buck warned, his ability to hold back his anger slipping dangerously.

"We should go," George suggested. He moved up alongside Lori. "We've all said enough tonight."

"I agree," Saul seconded. "We can discuss what, if anything, we're going to tell the media tomorrow when we've all gotten some rest. This has been an unbearable day."

Lori didn't look at Jenna as she left the room. George patted Jenna's arm as he passed, and made some quiet offering of apology. Saul said nothing.

When the front door had closed behind them, Buck heaved a weary breath. "I'm sorry you had to hear that."

"Why? It's true, isn't it? Everything she said. I couldn't deal with your life back then, why would now be any different?"

"Jenna." He moved toward her but she threw up her hands stop-sign fashion. "The past is over and done," he urged. "We don't need to rehash that painful time."

"Tell that to your team." She closed her eyes and shook her head. When she opened those weary eyes once more they were clear of the anger and pain. The emptiness there now was like a knife searing deep into his chest. "Not a single thing has changed. Your whole life still revolves around the team. What's best for the team. NASCAR. The rules. The media. You don't have room for a private life, Buck. Where would Becca and I fit into this world?"

He flared his hands, and didn't know what to say to her accusations. She wasn't being completely fair. What did she want from him? He was doing everything humanly possible to help. Didn't she see that?

"What do you want me to do, Jenna? Name it. I'll find a way to make it right."

A lone tear trickled down her cheek and her lips trembled into a sad smile. "Don't you see? You said almost that exact same thing to me thirteen years ago?" A sob visibly shook her. "Nothing has changed, Buck. You're a good man, but racing is your life. Your team is never going to accept me or my daughter because we're not like them. Our lives don't revolve around what you do. And that's okay." She swiped at her cheek with the back of her hand. "I got over all that a long time ago. But don't expect me to want to go through it again. I won't. And I damn sure won't put my daughter through it."

How did he make her see that he wanted to make all that change for her? But she wasn't finished yet. He held his tongue until she'd had her say.

She drew in a sharp breath and let it out slowly and

went on. "Tell me, Buck, until you learned that Becca was your child, can you truthfully say to me that you'd even considered having a child?"

Nothing she could have said would have damaged him more. "It's true, I didn't think I wanted kids. But I have a daughter. That changes everything. Do you really believe I'm the kind of man who would put business before his family obligations, Jen? Is that how you see me?"

"That's just it." Her voice quavered. "It's not about how I saw you then or how I see you now. There's a saying, Buck. Actions speak louder than words. Your people surrounded you tonight and they wanted you to put out a statement naming me and my daughter as the unexpected trouble in your life. You can paint it any way you want to, but that's what it boils down to."

"And you heard me say no," he argued, some of the fight going out of him at the idea that she would think for even a second that he would go along with that idea.

"You did." Another of those sad smiles bent her lips. "And I appreciate that. But this is the way it was back then and it's the way it would be now if Becca and I were involved with your life now. There would always be something." She shook her head slowly from side to side. "We don't fit in, Buck. We're not part of what makes you tick and the racing over-whelms all else. No matter how hard you try to include us, it will always be us against them. Our presence would only tear you and the people who mean so much to you apart. I won't be a party to it. I can't hurt you like that. That's why I walked away before, it's why I'll do the same this time." A barely discernible shrug lifted her shoulders. "It's the only thing I can do."

He watched her turn and walk away. The right words to respond to all that she'd said eluded him completely. The notion that she'd left him in part because she felt she didn't fit in, because she hadn't wanted to cause division among his team, shattered something deep inside him. He couldn't name it…he only knew that the pain was paralyzing.

He'd lost her…had lost all those years with his daughter because he'd been a blind fool who, evidently, couldn't see past his own needs.

Why had it taken thirteen years and a devastating tragedy to see that?

The worst part of all was that it might be too late to make any of it right.

CHAPTER ELEVEN

JENNA LEANED AGAINST the tile wall of the shower until the water ran cold. She'd cried until there were no more tears. She felt empty now, hollow and impotent.

She kept seeing the blood spatters on the money. And that body bag. Every muscle in her body clenched at the memory. What kind of man used something like that to hurt another human being?

And the letter. She shuddered.

There are some things that money cannot buy.

He had not called again. She'd left her cell phone lying on the closed toilet lid to ensure she heard it if it rang.

Was the waiting part of his game?

She didn't know how much more she could take. She wanted to be strong for Becca, but she was only human.

She shivered as the coolness of the water penetrated her foggy thoughts, prompting her to shut off the cold spray. Her hair got a good toweling, she didn't have the energy to search for a blow dryer. Once she'd dried her skin, she wrapped a clean towel around her and shuffled to the bed. She didn't have a gown or nightshirt, the towel would just have to do. Sleep might be impossible, but she had to try. Exhaustion had already claimed every inch of her body and mind.

No more thinking.

She'd tried to call her mother but got the answering machine. This wasn't the kind of message she could leave on a machine. It wasn't like her mother not to be home this late, and the woman outright refused to carry a cell phone. Jenna would just have to try again later or early in the morning and hope she reached her before she saw the news.

Once Jenna crawled into bed, no matter how hard she tried, closing out the horror of her missing child and the ugly scene with Lori and the others proved impossible. Nothing had changed between her and the team. How could Buck expect Becca to want to be a part of that life when clearly his friends didn't want Jenna back? They were a package deal. Forget about it. Her daughter had grown up perfectly happy without a father. Jenna absolutely would not allow her to get attached to a man who could never put her first.

No way.

She knew all too well the lure of Buck's charisma. He was handsome and charming and rich. He was a celebrity and everyone around him lived in his glow...or in his shadow. She would not sentence her daughter to living in anyone's shadow. Becca would fall in love with her father only to have to learn the hard truth Jenna had already learned. Buck's heart belonged to racing.

Rolling onto her side, she tried to block the thoughts, ordered herself to sleep. The effort was futile.

He'd tricked her into caring about him when they had first met. Guilt pinged her. That wasn't a fair statement, but it wasn't exactly wrong, either. She hadn't had a clue he was a race car driver when she'd changed the sheets of his hospital bed that first time after his appendectomy. He'd let her start to fall in love with him without knowing all the facts. But she couldn't hold that against him, not really. He hadn't tried to seduce her. He'd been sweet and friendly, she just hadn't been able to resist him. He'd been young and following orders not to identify himself to anyone. He hadn't meant to mislead her. He'd hinted that there were things she didn't know, but that hadn't stopped her from plunging head over heels in love with him.

When she'd learned who he really was, she'd been startled and just a little terrified. He was a huge star even then. But he'd wooed her deeper into his life. And then she'd been hooked. The team had been startled as well. Their rising star just showed up one day with her in tow. A girl who knew absolutely nothing about stock car racing or NASCAR and who, admittedly, had much preferred it when she'd had Buck all to herself.

All those months she'd clung to the hope that at some point she would become first in his life. She would wait for him, just like the thousands of other fans, after a winning race. He would stride over to her, throw those strong arms around her and hug her tight. He looked so handsome in his racing suit…had smelled like the wind, wild and free. She had lived for those moments. But the moment would pass and then he would go back to being Buck Buchanan, the legend. The beloved driver.

After a while those moments hadn't been enough. She'd tried. Honestly, she had. She'd tried so damned hard to make it be enough. But she'd needed more and Buck couldn't give her any more. He gave everything he had to the sport…to the fans. Case in point, he hadn't even come after her when she'd walked away.

He hadn't wanted to hold on to their relationship badly enough to try and persuade her to come back.

Her mother had been right. She was better off without him in her life. That had been her mother's one and only comment after the breakup. It wasn't that she hadn't liked Buck, she simply understood what Jenna did…that it wouldn't work. She supposed it took someone who wasn't a part of the racing world to understand.

The other thing was the trouble with the team. If she was totally honest, she couldn't hold that part against Buck. Looking back, she'd often wondered if she had really wanted to fit in. She'd resented the massive chunks of time Buck had spent with the team and maybe she was jealous. She'd barely been twenty-two at the time. She'd grown up in a close family, a family who did everything together and none of it included such an all-consuming singular activity. She hadn't understood the dynamics. She'd balked at the overpowering scope of racing. She supposed Lori and some of the others had seen that as bad, considering Buck was their driver—the center of their racing universe.

Since Jenna hadn't wanted in, she had no doubt been seen as a distraction, a trouble spot. She supposed her somewhat uncooperative attitude had perpetuated the problem. Funny, she could look back and see that now. Maybe she was simply too tired to argue in her favor.

She'd really tried to fit in at times. The kickoff of that first season had been the best. She'd been awed by the relationship between Buck, the driver, and his fans. It was like being a groupie to a rock star. She'd initially been impressed by the extent to which people would go in the name of fandom. Then race time would near and the rumble of excitement in the grandstands would drop instantly to utter silence as tens of thousands stood for the National Anthem.

The moment the moving rendition ended and the order was given to start the engines, the earth literally shook as the crowd cheered in punctuation of the revving motors. The pace car would leave the track and the green flag would wave and the cars would shoot down the front stretch. The blur of colors and numbers made her shiver even now as she thought of the incredible speeds reached during the course of the race.

All those years ago, watching Buck's car, praying nothing would go wrong. She would listen in as the spotters and pit crew discussed problems and strategies with Buck as he flew around the track at upwards of one hundred and eighty miles per hour. Jenna had spent more time holding her breath during every race than she did breathing.

The near-misses were the hardest. She tugged the covers closer, shivering as she remembered. The blown engines and the spinouts that sent the cars and/or debris in Buck's path... She had been so proud of him as he'd deftly maneuver to avoid a collision while traveling at a rate of speed that boggled her mind.

No other sport came close to matching the intensity, the sheer exhilaration. She just hadn't been able to deal with the enormity of it. So she'd walked. She'd been thinking about it for a while and then, after learning she was pregnant, she just left.

Buck had just let her walk away without coming after her. In her mind, that was his answer to whether or not she came first.

She hadn't.

Fate had brought them back together in this nightmare. No matter that Buck was clearly putting her first right now, could she trust that wouldn't change once

Becca was back safe and sound? Daytona was around the corner. Would he head off and not look back?

But did she have the right to make that kind of decision, at this point, for her daughter?

For the past twelve years she had told herself that she'd made the right decision, that her daughter didn't need a father. Jenna had played both parts without a problem. Becca's grandmother was there as backup. What else did a child need? No one could point to any aspect of Becca's life so far and find it lacking.

But her little girl would be thirteen in a few months. Dating lurked right around the corner. Homecoming dances and proms. College and, eventually, a wedding. Those were all things where a father would come in handy. Even Jenna had to admit that. Becca's school district had father-daughter dances in high school.

As easy as it had been so far, that continuity was swiftly changing. But how did she tell her daughter that her father had been just down the road all along?

Would Becca hate her for keeping that secret? Probably.

The one thing Jenna knew with complete certainty was that if she could just get her daughter back unharmed, she would willingly walk barefoot across hot coals…she would face anything.

A soft rap on the door forced her eyes open. She sat up, shoved the hair out of her face. "Please go away, Buck." She didn't want to talk. Her emotions were too raw right now. She knew he would try to make things right. Try to smooth over the rough spots.

"I'm coming in," he warned.

She tugged the covers closer to her throat and pulled her knees up to her chest. Wearing nothing but the towel made her feel naked. With her hair wet and tangled she likely looked a mess.

The door opened and he walked in. He looked as if he'd had himself a shower, too. His hair was damp, his jaw clean shaven and the button-down shirt and jeans were crisp and fresh-looking. He looked so good…made her want desperately to allow him to comfort her the way only he could.

"Do you need anything else? Coffee? Brandy? Something to eat? I've got chili in the microwave."

"No, thank you. I don't need anything." She resisted the urge to run her fingers through her hair and attempt to put it in any kind of order.

He sat on the edge of the bed close to her feet. She wished he would just get it over with, say what he had to say and go. Being alone with him in this setting made her feel things she didn't need to feel. Memories she'd banished long ago kept trying to intrude. Hot, steamy memories that she had no business recalling.

"I wanted to tell you again how sorry I am about what Lori said. That conversation shouldn't have happened. I know she didn't mean to come off as un-feeling. She really is trying to help."

Jenna closed her eyes and fought the fatigue. "Buck, I know you're right, but I just don't want to talk about it anymore."

"Is that really why you left?"

Her eyes flew open. "What?" How the hell could he ask that question? He knew why she'd left.

"You thought I put the driving ahead of you?"

"Buck, how can you even ask? Don't you remember the arguments?" She wanted to throw her hands up, but since they were keeping the cover up around her shoulders she didn't. Instead it just made her very sad that after all of this time he still didn't understand. "You surely can't sit there and pretend you didn't put racing ahead of everything else in your life."

Racing wasn't a job to him, it was a way of life. Only the truly dedicated and genuinely talented made it to the top. Buck had been—still was—at the top.

Even if she hadn't gotten pregnant, she would have left eventually. She just couldn't take the extremes. She loved him—probably still did—but it was too hard. An emotional roller coaster.

He stared at the floor for a time, then he met her eyes once more and said, "I saw myself as dedicated and determined. I'll admit that the commitment is a little overwhelming at times, but it isn't that out of proportion. You make our relationship sound like it was all bad. Is that the way it felt to you?"

Dangerous territory. She had to tread carefully

here. "No, it wasn't all bad. We had moments." She moved her shoulders up and down in a vague shrug. "We had some really good moments. But you always went back to your first love, Buck. There was no place for me in the equation. Your racing friends didn't exactly invite me. I was the outsider. I lurked around in your shadow waiting for a moment of your attention. They ignored me, saw me as a distraction. Part of that was my fault, I admit it. But I can't believe you didn't see how it was."

The devastating look on his face told her how much her words pained him. "I didn't see it, Jen. Honest to God, I didn't."

"I don't want to hurt you, Buck. Let's just agree to disagree about the way we remember things."

Those brown eyes searched hers. "I am truly sorry I hurt you, Jen. Whatever my faults and deficiencies, I wish I could take them back somehow, make it right."

"You can't do over the past, Buck. That history is already written. We are who we are and what happened, happened. We live with our choices, right or wrong. I know I wasn't free of blame. I was selfish to want more of you to myself. You are who you are and I tried to change that. I was wrong. That's one reason I just let it go." She shook her head. "I guess it was just easier to blame you."

The confession startled her. The knowledge had always been there, she just hadn't said it out loud before.

Somehow he felt closer and yet she knew he hadn't moved. Maybe it was the intensity in those dark eyes.

"Do you ever wish you'd stayed? That you'd knocked me upside the head and made me understand how you felt?"

Surprisingly, laughter bubbled up in her throat. "That isn't a fair question, Buck." He really should go now. Her heart rate had steadily risen from the moment he walked through the door smelling of woodsy soap and looking entirely too vulnerable for the big, strong man she knew him to be.

"What's not fair about it?"

"Because it's just not."

His eyes appeared to be distracted by her lips now.

"Yes or no," he repeated. "It's simple. Do you ever wish—" his gaze locked with hers "—that you'd stuck it out?"

She wanted to lie. But she'd never been any good at lying. Avoiding a subject, she was great at that maneuver, but never lying.

"I've thought about it." That was as close to a yes as he was going to get. Now to turn the tables on him. "Do you ever wish you'd paid more attention to me when you had the chance?"

He winced. She'd hit her mark.

His recovery was instantaneous. He looked her straight in the eye and said, "Yes."

Those three little letters sent an earthquake of emotions rumbling through her. This conversation needed to end before they both did something they would regret.

"I've kicked myself a thousand times for not doing the right thing," he kept going. "Even though I can't say that I understood why you left, I should have come after you, and hounded you until I made you come back to me." The intensity in his eyes, in his expression, increased with every word. "I should have locked us in a room and made you tell me how you felt deep down. I should have made love to you—"

"Buck…" She pressed her fingers to her lips. "Please," she whispered, "stop." He made her wish for something that could never be…made her long to be in his arms like before…in those rare moments when it had been just the two of them.

"I won't let you walk away again, Jenna."

He made her shiver and he hadn't even touched her. "You…" She swallowed back the emotions crowding into her throat. "You can't stop me from going home when this is over. I won't stay."

"Maybe I can't, but I'll hang out on your doorstep every day. I won't give you a minute's peace until you agree to give us a second chance."

Us? Tears started to slip down her cheeks again. She had to stop falling apart like this. "There is no us, Buck."

"There's always been an us." His fingers dove into her hair and he tilted her face up to meet to his. "We were just stuck in denial, that's all."

His lips brushed hers and her heart lurched.

"I will not lose you twice in one lifetime, Jenna Williams." Another soft brush of his lips. "Be warned, you are in for the fight of your life."

And then he kissed her. He kissed her long and deep with all the skill she so vividly remembered. Buck Buchanan had always been a five-star kisser. Just the right amount of pressure…just the perfect blend of give-and-take.

His lips were so soft and at the same time firm, just like she remembered. His taste, tangy sweet like minty toothpaste. He'd planned to kiss her even before he came in here. Or maybe he'd hoped.

He lifted his lips from hers just far enough to allow a much-needed breath. She melted a little more at the electrifying sensation of him hovering so close after such an intense kiss.

"I was a fool, Jen. I won't make the same mistake twice."

It would be so easy to fall right into his arms and take up right where they'd left off all those years ago. But there was Becca to think of. She could not risk her being hurt.

"This is about more than just you and me this time." She drew back far enough to look into his brown eyes. The desire she saw there took her breath. He wanted her. Wanted her exactly the way she wanted him. But that would be a major mistake. Making love with Buck would terminate any possibility of rational thinking.

His thumb slid over her bottom lip, making her quiver with need. "I would never hurt that girl. Surely you know me better than that."

Reality intruded just a little more. "I know you would never intentionally hurt her. But your obligations—" she shook her head, leaned away from his touch "—they don't include a family, Buck."

He dropped his hands to the mattress, one on either side of her. "My profession does not exclude me from having a family, Jen. Lots of men in my position have a family. Plus things have changed. I'm the owner now, not a driver."

She inclined her head and considered his statement. "If that's so, then why aren't you married? I'm certain you've had plenty of opportunities since we parted ways. And keep in mind that you were the one who always said you didn't want children because of what your father did."

"Can't a guy be wrong?" he challenged. "And what about you? Have you been married?"

She held up her hands and moved them back and forth as if to erase the suggestion. "That doesn't count. I had a daughter to think of. I needed to focus on her, not on myself." She dropped her hands to her knees, knotted her fingers in the cover to prevent herself from touching him the way she foolishly wanted to.

He looked away. She'd expected as much. He couldn't possibly make her feel guilty for her choices. She had sacrificed her own happiness and her own needs many times for her daughter—and never regretted a second of it. Buck had never had to make a sacrifice for anyone. The entire subject reignited her anger at the memories. They should end this before feelings were hurt again.

"You want to know why I never married? Or even committed to a relationship after you?"

Anticipation sent her pulse into double time. "I think we've both said enough," she lied. As much as she wanted to hear what he had to say, she did not need to hear it. Some deeply ingrained instinct warned that whatever he told her would forever change something inside her and she couldn't allow that to happen. Couldn't permit the vulnerability that would no doubt accompany the change.

"I never wanted anyone else." He lifted those broad shoulders then let them fall. "Not once. A couple of dates was as far as any other relationship went." Those brown eyes trapped hers in their spell. "How could I want anyone else when I never stopped loving you?"

Before she could argue, he kissed her again. Harder this time, with a passion that would not be denied. Her heart pounded. Her body felt on fire. He kissed her until she was sure she would die of the overwhelming urgency to have more.

"I know you still have feelings for me, too," he murmured against her lips. "You can pretend all you want, but I know. I won't let go this time, Jen."

"Is that really what you want, Buck? Think long

and hard before you say those words to me." She looked into his eyes. "I don't want to go through that kind of hurt again," she whispered.

He kissed her again, slowly, tenderly. Then he whispered back, "You have my word."

She took control of the moment then. She'd restrained the need as long as she could bear it, then she just let go. She pushed him back onto the bed, sealed her lips over his. She wanted him. She needed him. Maybe she was a fool. God knew she'd sworn she would not let this happen, but she needed him too much to deny herself a minute longer.

The towel fell away and his clothes ended up on the floor. They made love the way she remembered. Age had only made them better.

IT WAS PAST MIDNIGHT and Jen couldn't sleep. She'd dozed off after they'd made love, but then she'd awakened and she just couldn't make her mind shut off again.

The moonlight and eerie glow from the exterior security lights filtered through the sheers on the windows, allowing her to study the man lying beside her. She didn't see how it was possible for him to be more handsome now than before. After all, they were both older. But he was…somehow. Maybe it was the maturity. He'd hit the big 4-0. He made love with the skill of a forty-year-old, but there wasn't a thing old about his stamina.

Jenna smiled, experienced a fierce bittersweet pang deep in her chest. How on God's green earth had she let this happen?

She'd needed some relief from the stress of the past thirty-six or so hours, that was true enough, but this…this was not a casual encounter. This was Buck. The man she'd loved for nearly half her life.

She stared at the ceiling and called herself every kind of fool. He'd told her flat out tonight that he wanted her back. How the heck was she supposed to deal with that? She'd certainly given him every indication that she was interested in the same. As she told Buck earlier, actions speak louder than words. Her cheeks burned at the idea that she'd been responsible for plenty of action in the past couple of hours.

There was no making this right. There would be consequences. But those would have to wait until after she had her daughter back.

The idea that she hadn't heard from the kidnapper in nearly twelve hours had her heart squeezing painfully. What if he never called again? What if…?

Stop. Stop. She couldn't torture herself that way. She had to believe. Had to be strong.

And how many times had she said that since about six Friday evening?

She didn't want to answer that one.

Despite the fact that she felt as if her prayers had been ignored, she prayed again. Maybe someone up there would be listening now.

Her cell phone erupted in the silence.

Her breath caught.

The bed shifted. "Is that him?" Buck demanded in a voice thick with sleep.

She grabbed her phone and stared at the screen. Her heart sank. Her mother.

"It's Mom."

Jenna rolled to her side, her back to Buck, and took the call.

"Jenna, what in God's name is going on? I just got home and there were five messages from friends and neighbors on my machine about tonight's news. Is it true?" Her voice wobbled. "Please tell me it isn't."

She should have thought of that. Her mother and her friends…the whole town would have seen the news tonight. Why hadn't she gone ahead and left a message?

"I tried to call," she said, her own voice quavering. "Where have you been?"

"It's Saturday. Did you forget my Red Hats club goes to dinner and a late movie?" Before Jenna could answer, her mother urged, "You're not answering my question. What's going on?"

"I didn't want you to worry," Jenna explained, the need to confide her every fear a powerful longing in her chest. "This has been a nightmare. There hasn't been a lot of time to do anything but focus on this madman and his crazy game. I should have tried to call you again or just gone ahead and left a message. I'm sorry, Mom."

"So it's true." Her mother's voice filled with tears. "Some evil man has got our girl?"

Emotions welled and it was all Jenna could do to keep her voice steady. "Yes. The police are doing all they can. Buck gave the ransom money but we still haven't gotten her back." She left out all the parts that would only worry her mother further.

"Sweet Jesus," Shirley Williams murmured brokenly. "How can this be?"

"We think it's an enemy of Buck's. Someone out to hurt him, using Becca."

Her mother's silence was answer enough as to how she felt about that.

"Mom, I shouldn't keep this line tied up. He could call back." She hated to give her own mother the brushoff, but the more they talked the more worked up they would both get. Neither of them needed that. "I'll call you the moment I hear anything. Please try not to get yourself upset. And Mom, pray, will you?"

Her mother said a quick, passionate prayer for her granddaughter's safe return. After a fervent *amen,* Jenna thanked her and reminded her mother that she loved her. She closed the phone and placed it back on the night table. The action seemed so ordinary, but there was absolutely nothing ordinary about any of this.

"Is your mother all right? Should you call someone to stay with her?"

That was an excellent idea. She could call Gina.

She'd probably heard the news as well…unless, of course, she was still otherwise indisposed with Dr. Dale. "You're right. I should make sure someone keeps an eye on her. This kind of stress could bring on trouble."

A burst of musical notes from Buck's cell phone filled the air. The sound ignited a new wave of tension in Jenna.

Buck rolled toward the table on his side of the bed and answered it. "Buchanan."

Jenna held her breath, listened in hopes of identifying the caller. It wouldn't be the kidnapper, he always called on her phone. The sheriff? Had they gotten the analysis on the blood?

Her pulse fluttered and the breath she'd been holding rushed out of her lungs in a surge of worry. She just didn't know if she could bear to hear the results.

When Buck finally closed his phone and turned to her, she knew the news was not good.

"The blood on the money is the same type as Becca's. But that doesn't mean it's hers," he added quickly.

"I'm a nurse," she returned curtly, emotion pressing against the wall of her chest. "I know that. But I also know that the money came from the kidnapper. The kidnapper has my daughter. That it belongs to her is the most logical conclusion."

Oh, God. Oh, God. Oh, God.

She closed her eyes, fought the storm of emotions.

"What can I do, Jenna? Anything, you name it."

She shook her head. "I just need to be alone for a few minutes. Okay?"

The pain on his face told her she'd hurt him but she just couldn't deal with anyone else's emotions right now.

"I'll go…make some hot cocoa. That might make you feel better."

He sat up and pulled on his jeans. When he'd walked out and closed the door behind him, she let the floodgates open.

She cried so hard that the sobs were physically painful. God, how could she go on without her child? She couldn't. She couldn't.

Please, please, let her be okay.

Why was she praying?

Her eyes snapped open. She viciously swiped her cheeks with the backs of her hands. That hadn't done a damned bit of good.

There had to be something she could do!

She couldn't just sit here waiting!

Did she dare attempt to call her daughter's cell number?

The sound that shattered the aching silence sent her heart into a gallop. *Her cell phone.*

Before she got her hopes up, she reminded herself it could be Gina. She may have seen the news. Or her mother calling again.

Jenna swiveled her head, stared down at the phone

lying on the table. The screen lit up with another ring. Her hand reached for it, the movement surreal…slow motion almost.

She stared at the screen.

It was him.

Her heart rate surged into hyperspeed.

She opened it. "Hello."

"Mommy?"

Jenna gasped, her heart thudded. "Bec?"

"Mommy, please come get me. I'm scared."

CHAPTER TWELVE

"BABY, WHERE ARE YOU? I'll come and get you right now."

"Hello, Jenna."

Fear and anger roared like a cyclone. "Where's my little girl, you son of a bitch?"

"Didn't you hear? She wants you to come and pick her up. She's tired of my company. If you do exactly as I tell you, you'll have her back within the hour."

A feeble hope bloomed in her chest. "Just tell me what to do." Her breath hitched. She would do anything. Anything he asked.

"As I'm sure you've already concluded, the business I have is with Buck Buchanan, not with you."

She held onto the phone, wished she could hear her baby's voice again. "Yes," she choked out.

"I've decided that you and your daughter have served your purpose. You are to come to the Maple Hill Cemetery, the main entrance. Your daughter will be waiting for you there. The two of you can go home. You are no longer a part of my game."

There had to be a catch. "I can come now?" Please, please let him say yes.

"You may come in thirty minutes. If you leave Hampton Cove within the next ten to fifteen minutes you will have plenty of time."

"I'm on my way."

"Not so fast, Ms. Williams."

The heat of anticipation cooled as if a second ice age had descended. "What? You said I could come and get her."

"You can. Yes. You surely can. But you must come alone. If you do not come alone, I will be very angry. If I get angry, I can't make any guarantees about your daughter's welfare."

"I'll come alone. I swear." Even as she made the promise she wasn't sure how she would make it happen. Buck was keeping a pretty close eye on her.

The connection dropped off and Jenna closed her phone.

Since she didn't have any other clothes, putting her jeans and sweater back on wouldn't seem strange. She threw off the covers and rushed into the en suite bath. When she'd washed up a little, she quickly dressed.

Buck would be down in the kitchen making the cocoa. She could pretend she'd changed her mind about having a cup. Then what?

Giddiness at the idea of having her daughter back made her shiver. Her baby was alive and okay.

She'd heard her voice. She was going to get her back. Tonight.

But first she had to get there. Alone.

She shoved her phone into the hip pocket of her jeans and headed downstairs. The smell of fresh-brewed coffee had her stomach rumbling. Apparently he'd decided to make coffee as well. Maybe a sip or two before she slipped away would do her good.

"You decided to come down after all?" He set his mug aside and reached for a clean one for her.

He looked amazing. Rumpled and sexy.

"The smell of your coffee lured me."

"There's cocoa, too."

"Coffee."

He handed her a steaming cup. "I know you're worried about the results of the analysis."

She nodded, sipped her coffee. "I'm dealing with it." Don't let him see the lie. If he sensed any hint of what she had planned, he wouldn't allow her out of his sight.

Time was ticking by. How was she going to escape his watchful eye?

She couldn't.

She needed a distraction.

The reporters.

That could work.

"I think I'll take this upstairs with me." She took another sip. Made an appreciative sound.

"You need some company?"

The hopeful look on his face made a part of her

yearn to say yes. "I think I'd like to try and get some rest." She held up the coffee mug. "If the caffeine doesn't send too much of a shock through my system."

"Let me know if you need anything."

She had to get out of here before she broke down and told him about the call. As much as she wanted to tell Buck, she knew he would insist on going with her. She'd sworn she would come alone. That was the deal. Plain old common sense warned her that it could be a trap. But trap or no, she couldn't take any chances with her daughter's life. She just couldn't.

Just like Buck said before, they had to play by this madman's rules. There were no other options.

Once closed away in the guestroom, she called information and got the number for the county sheriff's department. When dispatch answered she said, "This is Jenna Williams. Two or more of your deputies are stationed outside my location. Buck Buchanan's house." She gave the address.

"Yes, ma'am, how can I assist you?"

Jenna held her breath and hoped like everything this would work. "Could you patch me through to one of the deputies outside? I need to speak with one of them. It's urgent."

"One moment, ma'am."

If this didn't work she'd have to try a flat-out run for it. What was the code for the security system? Something simple. Oh, yeah, No. 86, the race car. 8686.

"This is Deputy Grider, how can I help you, Ms. Williams?"

She squared her shoulders, refused to let his authoritative tone intimidate her. "I'm sorry to bother you, deputy, but I've decided to make a statement to the press. A plea for my daughter's return. I'm sure you understand what I mean. Could you please permit the reporters to come to the front door? No vehicles, just the reporters and their cameramen." She didn't want the vehicles blocking the drive.

"Are you sure about that, ma'am? Maybe I should speak with Mr. Buchanan."

"Deputy Grider? Is that your name?"

He cleared his throat. "Yes, ma'am."

"Buck is standing right next to me. Do you want to verify that I'm telling the truth?" The lie left a bitter taste on her tongue. That it rolled off so easily was a testament to her desperation.

"No, ma'am. I guess not. We'll send in the reporters." Hesitation. "You sure you want all of 'em?"

"Yes, Deputy Grider, send all of them. Might as well get it over with all at once."

Now, she had to get into position. She shoved the phone back into her pocket. Wondered where the heck her purse was but decided she didn't need it. She'd left the keys in her Bug when she'd first arrived. She hadn't been in it since. The keys should still be in the ignition.

In the kitchen there was a door that went into a

laundry room. The door to the garage was there, as well as a door to the backyard. That was the one she wanted.

First things first.

She stole out of the room and moved noiselessly down the stairs. She could hear Buck speaking to someone. He was still in the kitchen.

What if the sheriff's office had decided to call and confirm her request to send in the reporters?

God, what would she do then?

The doorbell chimed and her heart bumped hard against her rib cage. She dashed around the newel post and flattened against the wall next to the closet door. When Buck came into the entryhall from the kitchen his profile would be to her and his attention would be on the door…she hoped.

The doorbell rang again just as he exited the kitchen, which assured that his attention was fully focused on the door as he went to see who would show up at this hour. Maybe someone up above was looking out for her after all.

He peered through the security peephole. "What in blazes?" He entered the security code, swung the door open and quickly stepped out onto the porch, pulling the door closed behind him.

He'd done that last part to protect her. She should feel rotten. But she couldn't. Her daughter was waiting for her. She had to focus on that single goal.

She rushed through the kitchen and out the door leading to the backyard. Taking care not to make any noise, she made her way around the side of the house. The crowd of reporters had gathered around Buck on the porch that spanned the length of the front of the house, effectively blocking him from view. This was good.

If they would just stay like that for two or three more minutes, she would be set.

All she had to do was stay in the shadows at the edge of the yard until she reached her car about midway down the drive.

Jenna didn't take another breath until she was at her car. She ducked down when a squad car rolled up the driveway. Evidently Buck had demanded that the deputies come and clear the crowd. He would be fired up when he discovered what she'd done.

She had to move now. She opened the door and slid behind the wheel. Without turning on her headlights, she started the ancient Bug and shifted into Reverse. Keeping an eye on the crowd as well as the squad car, she rolled out onto the street. The other squad car stationed on the street and the two deputies there didn't give chase as she drove away. She was pretty sure they'd noticed her departure, but they didn't do anything about it.

She drove as fast as she dared. Her purse was missing in action, which meant she didn't have her driver's license, so she couldn't risk being stopped for speeding.

The ten minutes required to drive over the

mountain into Huntsville was the longest she'd ever lived. She estimated ten more minutes to the Five Points area and the cemetery. She would just make it.

By the time she reached the final intersection before the historic Maple Hill cemetery, the tears had started to glide down her cheeks. She told herself not to cry. But the idea of seeing her little girl again, of holding her, overwhelmed her. She just couldn't help it. The tears flowed.

She turned down the street that would take her to the main entrance. Slowing to a near stop, she eased into the narrow lane that wound through the cemetery. She wasn't sure how far she should go so she parked just inside the gate and got out of the car.

It was illegal to be in the cemetery after dark. She shivered as she looked across the rows of ancient tombstones. Not exactly any place she would want to be at night under normal circumstances. The idea that Bec would be terrified in a place like this sent an ache stabbing through her.

"Becca!" she shouted as she got out of the car. She couldn't help herself.

"Mom!"

Her heart reacted.

"I'm coming, baby!"

To her right. Beyond a monstrosity of a private crypt. Her daughter! Standing all alone in the dark. Jenna ran. She stumbled, caught herself a split second before hitting the ground and kept plunging ahead.

She was here. Her little girl was really here.

All she had to do was reach her. Throw her arms around her and take her home.

The blow came from behind.

A jarring jolt to the back of her skull.

The ground flew up to meet her.

The blackness stole her next thought.

CHAPTER THIRTEEN

"BUCK! CAN YOU TELL US why you've kept your daughter a secret all this time?"

Buck had done this hundreds of times, faced an unexpected throng of newshounds. It wasn't a big deal. He appreciated the media's attention. As long as it was on him, it wasn't on someone else.

But this time was different. This time he couldn't find the right words to say to answer a single question. Even as two deputies worked to disperse the group of reporters, questions he couldn't answer were flung at him.

"Were you afraid something like this might happen?"

He stepped back inside his house and closed the door against the unsettling scene outside.

That last question reverberated inside his head as he sagged against the door.

Was this part of the reason Jenna had kept Becca away? Had she feared her daughter would become a target someday if her link to him was known? He was a very rich man. And rich men had enemies.

Buck understood that some amount of risk was involved with his celebrity status. God knew there were a lot of desperate people in this world. He'd been in the limelight so long now that he'd grown complacent when it came to the idea of being a target.

But then he hadn't had a daughter to worry about until now. That was the difference.

As a grown man living in the spotlight he'd never felt the fear, never worried about the possibilities. But a child couldn't protect herself. The idea that this child was his own, that she was not merely a theory or a possibility, made taking his next breath a chore.

He'd always sworn he wouldn't have children. He couldn't bear the idea of anything he did or didn't do making a child unhappy or miserable, as he had been as a kid. In the beginning it had been mostly about his no-good daddy, but then he'd realized he didn't have the time necessary for that kind of commitment. So he'd stuck by his initial decision.

Yet, here he was, the cause of pain to a child, his child. The thought twisted inside him.

For the last thirty-some hours he had pretended that he had everything under control. He was Buck Buchanan, after all. He got things done. He wasn't afraid of anything. Not once in his racing career had he backed down from a challenge or run from the fire. He'd never failed to accomplish his goal.

What if he failed this time?

Would anything he did be enough?

The answer was abundantly clear.

His opponent had already proven who was in control and it wasn't Buck, leaving him no choice but to react.

There was no guarantee they would even hear from the kidnapper again.

They might never find that little girl.

His little girl.

The fear took hold deep inside...tore at his heart.

How the hell did he make this right?

He didn't let the son of a bitch win. That was what he did. The fire of determination ignited in him. He reached into his pocket for his phone. Time to check in with George and see what he'd found on McElroy. He needed to act instead of waiting to react.

A knock on the door behind him dragged his attention there. He slid his phone back into his pocket and checked the security peephole to find the reporters gone and one of the sheriff's deputies waiting on the porch.

Buck opened the door. "Thank you for handling that situation so quickly."

The deputy looked uncertain how to proceed. "Sir, I'm sure sorry about the misunderstanding. But I spoke with Ms. Williams personally. Or at least the woman who called identified herself as Jenna Williams. She insisted that I allow the reporters onto the property since she wanted to make a statement. A plea, she called it, for her daughter's safe return."

Buck understood the deputy's confusion. He was damned confused himself. "Obviously, the woman who called you was an impostor." Jenna was upstairs in bed, probably asleep by now. God knew she needed some relief and sleep was the only way to find any in this nightmare.

"We won't let it happen again, Mr. Buchanan. Sorry for the trouble."

When the deputy had joined his partner and driven back out to the street to maintain the necessary vigil, Buck closed the door and activated the alarm once more.

Like any other field, there were a few in the media who would go to any lengths to get the interview they sought or the story that might make their career. The idea that someone would have utilized such underhanded methods at a time like this was not completely outside the realm of possibility.

But it felt wrong. Buck knew most of those folks. They were just doing their jobs. He couldn't see one of them stooping that low.

He climbed the stairs with the intention of checking on Jenna…just to be sure.

The sheriff's warning about keeping him informed of their every move reverberated inside him. Surely she wouldn't have gone against that advice.

By the time he reached the guestroom where he'd left Jenna resting, he had a bad, bad feeling.

He knocked. "Jenna, we need to talk."

No answer.

"I'm coming in."

He opened the door and found the bed empty.

The tangled mass of sheets reminded him of what they'd shared in this room only a few hours ago. His gut clenched when he thought of the mistake he'd made by ever having let her go. He should have tried harder.

"Jenna?"

He checked the en suite bath. Not there.

Her clothes were gone. The towel she'd abandoned earlier lay on the floor.

The panic started its slow creep up his spine. He checked every room upstairs and then those downstairs before he gave up and admitted the truth.

She was gone.

She'd pulled a fast one on him. And he didn't have to ask himself why.

Another call had come. Whatever bait that scumbag had dangled, she'd taken it, hook, line and sinker.

Buck understood her desperation. He couldn't claim to know exactly how she felt, but he was certain she would do anything to save her child.

He went outside, checked for her Bug. Sure enough, it was gone. She was gone.

No denying that any longer. The only question left was, what did he do about it? Finding her would be impossible. He didn't have a clue where to start. He could wait or he could do the right thing.

He chose to do the right thing. He pulled out his cell and called Sheriff Sykes. Buck couldn't fight this man alone. There was no denying that any longer, not after discovering the money splattered with the child's blood. The police were trained in these matters, but they couldn't move forward blindly.

THE NIGHT HAD BLOOMED into dawn before Buck got the news.

Jenna's abandoned car had been found at Maple Hill Cemetery. Her cell phone had been discovered in the grass near a mausoleum. No sign of her or her daughter.

He emerged from his Escalade and joined the search at the cemetery.

Sykes met him at Jenna's Bug.

"Still nothing?"

The sheriff shook his head. "We've got the Huntsville Police Department working with us out here but I don't think we're going to find anything."

Buck surveyed the cemetery, the largest and oldest one in the state. It went on for nearly one hundred acres. Huntsville's city police had brought the K-9 patrol. Maybe they would pick up Jenna's scent.

"Do you remember what time you spoke with or saw her last?" Sykes wanted to know.

Buck nodded. That one was easy. They'd just made love and were lying in bed together. "You called with the news about the match on the blood type."

Sykes considered his response. "Is it possible," he asked, "that hearing that news caused her to go into hiding? Maybe run away from reality? The stress may have gotten to her."

That was something Buck hadn't considered. Mainly because he knew Jenna would not run away when her child was missing.

"She's a nurse," he told Sykes. "She deals with stressful situations every day."

"She's still human, Buck. This is her child we're talking about, not a patient who rolled in off the street."

"I see your point," Buck admitted. He felt sick to his stomach. How had he let her slip right out from under his nose? "But I know this woman. She would never do anything to endanger her child's life. Maybe if you hadn't found her phone here, maybe then I might consider that possibility. But there's no way she would do anything that might sever her connection to her daughter."

No way.

"All right then." Sykes surveyed the cemetery where his men worked jointly with HPD in hopes of finding some indication of what might have happened. His gaze locked with Buck's once more. "We'll treat Jenna as our second victim in this case."

The media had arrived in force and were taking up positions around two sides of the cemetery. HPD kept them as far behind the yellow tape, marking the area as a crime scene, as possible but the right kind of zoom lens would put a good photographer right in the thick of things.

Buck felt more tired than he had in his life. He closed his eyes and exhaled a weary breath. Who was doing this?

George hadn't found anything. As a side note, he'd mentioned that Reed was already in Daytona, gearing up for the first race of the season with his new team. And McElroy was conveniently out of the country. Vacationing abroad, his brother had said. George was working to confirm that McElroy was in fact thousands of miles away.

In other words, they had nothing.

Shouting in the distance drew Buck's weary attention across the pre-Civil War cemetery. Several officers had converged around one headstone in particular. Sykes jogged in that direction. Before he'd realized he was moving, Buck had started heading that way as well.

His heart pounded harder with every step he took. He wanted to break into a run but fear held him back. He wasn't sure he could bear to see what he might find.

When he reached the location, Sykes met him on the fringes of the small crowd of officers gathered.

"He's left a message for you, Buck."

Buck nodded and followed Sykes beyond the circle of uniforms.

A piece of cardboard had been cut to the size and shape of the headstone against which it rested. The message written in bold letters read:

Here Lies Buck Buchanan
A Man Who Has Outlived His Purpose

"You don't have any idea who might be behind this?" Sykes pressed. "This isn't just some random act. Whoever is doing this feels justified in his actions, Buck. Has reason to feel strongly about revenge."

Buck wasn't sure the police could dig up anything his people hadn't found already, but there was always a chance. "Tom McElroy."

"McElroy?" Sykes looked dumbfounded. "You and Tom have been friends a lifetime."

Buck nodded. That was true. He met Sykes's eyes. "I don't want to go into the details, but if this is about me, which clearly it is—" he looked down at the faux headstone "—then it has to be Tom."

Sykes nodded. "Then that's the direction we'll take our investigation." He looked back at the street. "You should go home, Buck. There's nothing else you can do here. The longer your face is within range of one of those cameras, we're going to have reporters attempting to figure out what we're doing out here."

Right again.

Buck thanked him for all that he and his men were doing. Sykes assured him he would keep him informed. He warned Buck again to stay close to home and to keep his men informed of his movements and/or any calls he received.

With one last glance at the threat on the headstone,

Buck made his way back to his SUV. His leather coat didn't keep the chill of the February morning at bay but he doubted that anything would. He felt numb from the inside out.

It took four officers to keep the reporters back long enough for him to climb into his vehicle and pull away from the curb near the cemetery's entrance.

He followed Lowe Street, eventually turning in the direction he needed. His movements were mechanical, mindless. The worst that could happen had.

His daughter, a child he'd never even met, was missing. And now Jenna.

Any pain, physical or mental, those two suffered would be his fault.

This was about him.

And they were paying the price.

Fury detonated, obliterating the softer emotions that made him feel powerless and lost.

This bastard wanted something. If not money, what?

That was the key. Not even a madman would go to all this trouble for nothing.

If he'd understood the epitaph back there, the only thing this man wanted was Buck dead.

A Man Who Has Outlived His Purpose.

Outlived his purpose…the phrase kept echoing in Buck's head. Lombardo was in a wheelchair, his once action-filled life now impotent. His association with NASCAR was gone, history…making all he'd ever worked for pointless. Maybe that epitaph was about the author as well as Buck. He couldn't risk that he'd been wrong to rule out Lombardo so quickly. He fished for his cell phone and put in a call to George. "I could be wrong about Lombardo," he said the instant George answered. "Look at him a little harder. Something isn't right about that message the kidnapper left me." Buck couldn't be sure... couldn't put his finger on precisely what he felt. "Find whatever you can."

Buck focused his attention back on his driving.

More members of the media waited at the end of his drive. Cameras flashed and questions were shouted at him as he made the turn. It was the first time he'd ever truly resented the intrusion. He needed to think. To find some place in his mind where he could analyze this pain he felt.

He desperately needed to figure out which of his two enemies had been willing to risk prison time to hurt him.

Buck parked in the garage and went inside, taking care of the security system by rote.

The house was quiet. Too quiet.

That feeling of being alone hit him hard, harder than before.

He walked upstairs and went into the room where he and Jenna had made love. He touched the pillow where she'd lain, then sank onto the mattress and wondered how he could have done things differently. How he could have made her stay.

Maybe he hadn't shown her enough attention but that didn't mean she hadn't been a part of his every thought. Win or lose, she was always the first person he sought out after crossing that finish line. The moment the car stopped and the engine died, his full attention was focused on her. She'd fly into his arms and that was the moment that made everything worth the effort. Even as he took care of the fans and business, she was still on his mind. Why hadn't he been able to show her that truth?

It was too late for those questions now. Like she'd said, you can't redo the past.

The future was a different story. He wanted to write it differently. But somebody intended to stop him from having that opportunity, from sharing his life with Jenna and their daughter. How the hell had McElroy or Lombardo learned the truth when he hadn't even known?

Evidently one of those two had been looking for a way to get at him. Anyone who'd known him and Jenna before would only have to see the child and, as Jenna said, do the math to figure out the biology. Uncovering that fact had provided the means by which to get to him.

They'd found their opportunity in a little girl who wasn't guilty of a damned thing except inheriting the wrong genes.

His cell rang and his blood froze.

It could be *him.*

Buck jammed his hand into his pocket and grabbed the phone. He didn't bother looking at the number. "Buchanan."

"What the hell is going on, Buck?"

Lori.

Damn.

"Your face is all over the news. Why didn't you call me and let me help with this?"

The memory of the painful exchange between Lori and Jenna knotted his gut a little more tightly. "Lori, I'm not sure there's anything else you can do right now." He knew how that sounded. Hell, he was the first one to admit how the media could change a person's destiny. No one was more keenly aware of just how volatile that relationship could be.

The silence that dragged on too long told him he'd done damage he hadn't intended.

"Buck, this is very difficult and I understand that. But the situation is out of control," she said with far more calm than he'd expected. "But if you don't want me to do my job, say so and I'll back off right now."

Buck closed his eyes and struggled with his emotions. He hadn't felt this lost, this helpless, since…Jenna left the first time.

"Lori, I'm sorry." He exhaled a mighty breath. "You're right. I haven't allowed you to do your job." Determination solidified inside him, helping him fight the helpless vulnerability he felt. Buck Buchanan wasn't accustomed to understanding that particular emotion so thoroughly. "But we're going to change that right now."

He gave Lori her orders. She was to release a statement saying that Buck greatly appreciated the thoughts and prayers of everyone watching this tragedy play out.

"Tell them," Buck went on, "that when my daughter is safely home again that her mother and I will make a joint statement at which time I will gladly answer all their questions."

"You believe Jenna will go along with that?"

The edge in Lori's tone told him it could be a long time before that fence was mended. But they had to start somewhere.

"We'll cross that bridge when we come to it," he countered. "I won't go back on my word. I'll give the people the answers they deserve, whatever happens. Then tell them to get ready for Daytona because we intend to win."

Lori was satisfied with that answer.

He'd no sooner ended the call than the front doorbell chimed.

Buck hustled down the stairs. Sykes would have called if he'd had news.

Unless it was bad.

Then he would come in person.

That numbing chill he'd wrestled with all night took hold again as he hesitated at the door. He did not want this to be more bad news.

Taking a breath, he checked to see who waited on the other side of the door.

Reba.

Oh, hell. She looked madder than blazes.

He opened the door and she glared at him.

"You've got some explaining to do, Brother. Imagine my surprise when I got home this morning from my sales conference to find a message on my answering machine telling me the crazy story I'd just heard on the radio in the car was true. You couldn't call my cell phone?"

"You had it turned off when I tried," he countered, thankful he could cover that base. Reba was not one to be left out of the loop. He had to admit he had tried, but then the situation had simply gotten too out of control to think about calling her again.

She lifted one eyebrow higher than the other. "Oh. Well, in that case, I might let you off the hook."

Once he'd ushered his sister inside and they'd hugged, he settled her on the sofa. He made a fresh pot of coffee and filled her in on what she'd missed.

Sipping his second cup, he waited for Reba to have her say. That was the way it was with older sisters. You had to listen whether you wanted to or not.

"I can understand why Jenna chose not to tell you."

He'd been sure nothing his sister could say would surprise him but he'd been wrong. "What do you mean?"

"She was and is like me, Buck."

Now he was thoroughly confused.

"She loved you, probably still does. But you have always said you didn't want kids. Everyone knew that. We'd both made our feelings on the issue pretty damned clear. And I'm sure she understood your dedication to NASCAR but felt on the outside. Don't you understand that?"

He wasn't sure he did. But he wanted to.

"How do you propose I go about fixing that?" He wanted this problem resolved. He wanted to make it right.

"Do you really want my advice, Buck," she asked frankly, "or are you merely indulging me so I won't be angry with you for failing to track me down in Montgomery and let me know what was going on back here?"

Reba Buchanan Moody was not a woman easily fooled or charmed. No one knew that better than him. And though she was two years older, she looked young for her age and was nothing short of beautiful. Just like their mother had been. And she generally got her way.

He rose from his chair and joined her on the sofa. "Help me make this right, Reba. I don't want to make the same mistake again."

Reba smiled, her eyes watery. "Everything's going to be fine, Buck. We're all going to work together and turn this thing around."

He hugged his sister. Prayed she was right.

If he could just get Jenna and Becca back, he would do whatever was necessary to make them both happy.

His cell interrupted before Reba could rattle off her list of suggestions for improving his relationship skills.

Tension riffled through him as he drew away from his sister's caring embrace. "I have to take this, Reba. It could be Sykes calling with an update."

She reached for her coffee. "Do what you have to do. I'll enjoy my coffee before it gets any colder."

Buck fished the phone from his pocket and flipped it open. "Buchanan."

"Can you speak freely?"

Buck went still for three beats, then fury whipped through him. He resisted the impulse to threaten the kidnapper with what he intended to do when he got his hands on him. He couldn't afford a mistake.

"Absolutely," he said, infusing his tone with calm. He pushed to his feet and stepped away from the sofa. "You have an update for me?"

"Ah. Someone is in the room," the garbled voice suggested. "Perhaps it's that lovely sister of yours."

"That's right." A muscle in Buck's face started to flex with the escalating tension. How could he know their every move?

"Very well. It's not necessary that you respond. You need only listen."

Buck paused at the front window and adjusted the shutter so that he could see the police cruiser as well as the flock of media gathered at the street.

"You have my full attention," he assured.

"Jenna and Becca would like to go home," he said in that ugly, twisted voice. "Would you like to make that happen, Buchanan?"

He suppressed another wave of fury. "Yes." Even with his best efforts the one word came out loaded with rage.

"As you must be aware by now, I am not interested in your money."

Buck held on to his control a little more tightly. "Yes, I'm well aware of that."

"There really is only one thing I want."

"Name it," Buck returned without hesitation.

"You sound so sincere," the voice taunted. "I only wish it was that simple."

"It is that simple," Buck challenged.

"Very well then. What I require is something only you can give me. It must be done discreetly. You must come alone or the deal is off and the game is over. Both Jenna and Becca will die on the spot. No questions. No second chances. Do you understand?"

The fury he felt was abruptly diluted by fear. "Yes."

"As I said, I want only one thing."

Buck wanted to snarl at him. To demand that he get to the point, but he held himself back, didn't lash out. "What do you want? Tell me and we'll get this done."

"You."

No surprise.

"When and where?" That was all Buck needed to know.

"Wait until dark. Go to the Buchanan Building. A car will be waiting."

Buck glanced at his sister to ensure nothing he'd said had attracted her attention. "No problem."

"Excellent. Remember, you must come alone. This is the final lap, Buchanan. If you make a single mistake, you forfeit and they both die. The game ends with this move. Don't screw it up. I've waited a very long time for this moment. And when it comes you will know how it feels to lose *everything*."

Buck tensed. "I'm fully aware of what's at stake."

"I sincerely hope so," the vile voice reiterated. "I would hate to tell Becca that she has to die because her daddy failed her. She's counting on you, Buck. Don't let your little girl down the way your father let you down."

Buck swallowed back the threatening words that rushed into his throat. He wanted to tell this SOB just what he'd do if he harmed one hair on Jenna's or Becca's head. "I won't," he said instead.

The connection broke.

Buck closed the phone and tucked it back into his pocket.

Fear, anger and determination pressed against him from the inside, jeopardizing his ability to stay calm.

He had to remain fully composed.

If this man was watching, listening, anything he did or said could get Jenna and Becca killed.

Sheriff Sykes's warning echoed inside him.

Buck had to do this exactly as ordered—he had little choice. This SOB had left him with no breathing room, much less any options.

Except for one.

Teamwork.

Folks who didn't understand the sport of racing, who hadn't lived the NASCAR culture, didn't understand the complex workings of the team. The driver was the man out front in the limelight, but every single member, from the sponsor to the spotter, was required to make a safe win possible.

No one did it alone.

He turned to face his sister and shook his head. "Nervous sponsor. You'd think his world was coming to an end." The words said jokingly reverberated inside Buck with a somberness that threatened the chokehold he held on his emotions.

Buck walked over to the bar. "I need some seltzer water. Want any?"

"No thanks, I'm still enjoying my coffee." She held the cup in both hands as if she relished the warmth.

He filled a glass and set the bottle aside. "So what was that list of suggestions you were going to give me?"

As his sister launched into her ideas on how to fix things between him and Jenna, Buck quickly scrib-

bled a note on a napkin. The first line was a warning:
Do not react. Just do this!

"Sounds easy," he said when she paused for a breath.

He picked up his water, the bottle and an extra
glass, and walked over to join his sister on the sofa.
"I brought you a glass just in case you change your
mind." He sat his own glass on the table, before
handing Reba an empty one along with the napkin.
"You sure you don't want some?"

"No thanks…I'm good." Her breath caught softly
as she read the words on the napkin.

"All right, what comes after *buy her flowers on a
regular and unexpected basis?*" he asked, drawing
her attention back to him and praying she would be
able to do this without demanding answers.

She blinked and licked her lips as if fear had stolen
her ability to speak. "Well, of course…you should
take her out at least once a week. Date night. That's
a cardinal rule, don't forget that one." She managed
a stiff smile, her eyes wide with fear and confusion.
"Lowell has been banished to the sofa many times
over that one."

Buck chuckled, a sound he hoped passed for the
real thing. "I'll have to remember that one for sure."

It would be dark in a few hours and he had to trust
that his sister would do what had to be done just like
any other member of his team.

But he couldn't say a word.

CHAPTER FOURTEEN

"MOM."

Jenna felt her body shaking. She wanted to wake up but she couldn't. Something thick and fuzzy was wrapped around her brain. She tried to push past it…to open her eyes.

"Mom," the voice whispered urgently. "Wake up. Please wake up."

The voice was Bec's…she wanted her to wake up. To open her eyes. She kept saying so, over and over.

Jenna tried harder. Her daughter needed her.

Her lids fluttered. An image faded in and out of focus.

"Mom, you have to wake up."

Open, dammit, Jenna willed. Her lids cracked open, managed to maintain that narrow slit for a few seconds.

"Bec?" Jenna licked her lips. Her mouth was dry. She felt cold and weak. Her muscles didn't seem to want to respond to her demands to act. It was really her…her baby was right her with her. Alive….

"Are you okay, Mom?"

Her daughter was hovering over her, Jenna realized. Worry pinching her pretty face.

"Bec...where..." Jenna turned her head to look around. Pain crashed inside her skull and she cringed.

"Maybe you shouldn't move," Bec whispered. "He hit you pretty hard."

Jenna opened her eyes again and this time the dimly lit room spun wildly for about five seconds.

"I need to get up." Jenna braced her hands against the cold floor and tried to push herself up. She wasn't entirely successful.

Becca helped her then. She supported her mother's shoulders. "He gave you a shot of something to keep you asleep," she whispered. "He promised you'd be okay, but I was really scared."

He.

Her daughter's kidnapper.

A powerful mix of fury and determination surged through Jenna and she sat up the rest of the way. Closing her eyes against the spinning for a moment, she managed to slow the momentum then open them, settling her gaze on Becca.

"You're all right?" Tears gathered behind her eyes and it was all Jenna could do to hold back the sobs that rose in her throat. Bec was okay. And she was *here.*

Becca nodded. "I wanna go home."

Jenna grabbed her baby girl and held her close to her chest. "He didn't hurt you?"

Becca shook her head.

Jenna pulled her face up so that she could look directly into her eyes. "You've had food and water?"

Becca nodded.

Thank God. Bec looked all right. No visible bruises. Her white tee was no longer white and her face was streaked with dirt, probably from crying. Jenna thought about the blood she'd seen on the money…the same type as Becca.

"You're sure he didn't hurt you?"

Bec held out her arm, pointed to a Band-Aid at the bend of her elbow. "They took blood. That was the only thing that hurt."

Jenna shuddered. The man who'd taken her daughter truly was sick. She looked around, tried to analyze the situation. "Where are we? Could you see where he brought us?"

"A basement, I think. I'm not sure. I couldn't see. They made me wear the bag again."

Jenna's gaze settled on her daughter once more. "Can you tell me what the man who took you looked like?" Whatever he'd put over her daughter's head, he couldn't have done it until after he'd gotten her in the car.

"The first man had black hair and he was big." She bit her lip. "He told me he was a policeman and showed me a badge."

Surely that wasn't right? A policeman wouldn't be involved in something like this. "He wore a uniform?"

Becca shook her head. "No. A suit, like the detectives on TV. He came to the school after soccer practice and called me over to his car. He said you'd been in an accident."

Fear knotted in Jenna's stomach. "But he wasn't in a police car?"

She shook her head again. "I don't remember the car. Maybe it was brown or tan. He called my name and told me you'd sent him to bring me to the hospital."

Jenna felt ill. How many times had she and her daughter talked about that very scenario? It wouldn't do any good to bring that up right now. Later, when this was all behind them, they would revisit the subject of trusting strangers.

"Once we got out of town," she went on, her voice shaky, "he made me put a bag over my head so I couldn't see anything. He kept saying how sorry he was that he had to do it."

Like Calvin Hastings, Jenna realized. She didn't have to guess. She knew. The man had been coerced. She shuddered. To take a child…what on earth could this madman have used to force anyone to do that?

"I had to wear the bag again when we went to the cemetery to get you." Becca's lips quivered. "I thought he'd killed you when you got hit, but he promised you'd be okay."

Jenna wanted to kill the man responsible for this nightmare. The rage was almost overpowering. She hugged her girl. "I'm fine. Everything's going to be fine." She fought hard to maintain her composure. She didn't want to scare her daughter by losing control. All that really mattered was that she was okay.

"Mom," Becca said. "It was a different man at the cemetery. Not the same one who picked me up at school. This one looked mean but he didn't say a word. He was real quiet."

Jenna didn't know what that meant. Another person who'd been coerced or a hireling? But she was sure about one thing. They had to get out of here. "We have to try to escape." She struggled to her feet.

Becca scrambled up and grabbed her mother's arm when she swayed. "It's okay," she insisted. "The man in the wheelchair told me that my dad was coming."

Buck...oh, God!

"What man in a wheelchair? When did he tell you this?" Jenna had to warn someone. She had to get her daughter out of here and she had to help Buck.

"When we came back from the cemetery. There was a man in a wheelchair who said we'd have to stay here until dark and then we'd get to go home."

"What did this man in the wheelchair look like?" An enemy of Buck's for sure.

Becca shrugged. "Gray hair. Real old. I hadn't seen him before this morning. He said his name was Addison."

Addison? *Addison Lombardo?* He was in a wheelchair. Jenna vaguely remembered something in the news about him and a big falling out with NASCAR several years back. Buck had been involved somehow. She just couldn't remember the details. It was not all that long after she and Buck broke up. She'd tried to block all those memories.

If this man wanted Buck badly enough to kidnap two people...that could only mean he intended to hurt him. No, he intended to kill him. It also meant that he was obviously insane. He couldn't possibly hope to get away with something like this.

Then again...he'd gotten away with it so far.

"Mom, was he telling the truth?"

Jenna hauled her attention back to her daughter. "What, honey?"

"Is my dad coming to save us?"

How did she answer that question?

The truth. It was past time she'd told her daughter everything.

But there was no time now for the full story.

"It's true, Bec," she said. "I'll tell you all about your father as soon as we're out of here. I promise." She took a deep breath and forged on with what had to be done. "I want you to think really hard. Did you hear or see anything else?"

"Just one thing I didn't understand," Bec said, her brow furrowed in confusion. "I heard the old gray-haired man talking to someone after they put us back in here. I couldn't see who he was talking to 'cause my eyes were closed. I was pretending to be asleep."

Jenna nodded for her to keep going.

"The old man asked two times if everything was ready." She looked at Jenna. "What do you think he was talking about?"

Before Jenna could answer the lock on the door rattled.

Becca's gaze collided with hers. "I think he's coming."

IT WAS GOOD AND DARK when Buck arrived at the Buchanan Building as specified. He parked his Escalade and got out, resisting the temptation to look around. He'd no sooner closed the door than a big black Hummer pulled up next to him.

The driver's side window powered down and the man wearing the ski mask ordered, "Get in."

Buck did as he was told, climbing in the back.

The vehicle roared off into the darkness, moving away from downtown Huntsville and eastward. The man in the passenger seat had twisted around just enough to keep an eye on Buck, and the weapon in his hand indicated he was prepared to do whatever necessary to ensure cooperation. Neither man spoke after the initial order to get in.

Taking Highway 72 east, the silent journey continued for fifteen or twenty minutes. Buck couldn't risk a single glance behind him for fear of giving away what he'd done. He considered asking about Jenna and Becca but he doubted that either of these two goons could or would give him an answer. He wasn't very familiar with the area they drove through now but he recognized the rural community as Ryland Pike. When the driver stopped at a gate leading to what was presumably the meeting place, the enemy's identity was confirmed for Buck. During that final call, the garbled voice had bragged that he'd waited a long time for this moment. Tom McElroy's betrayal had occurred just two months ago. Lombardo's many years ago. Lombardo had to be the scumbag behind this nightmare.

If Buck had needed any additional evidence, the residence that sat atop a hill far above this road gave him just that. A towering iron fence rolled out around the property for as far as he could see with nothing more than the moonlight to aid him. A massive gate with accompanying cameras discouraged would-be intruders.

Lombardo was an extremely wealthy man. He could very well own a number of prime pieces of real estate, including this one. Conversely, this was way out of McElroy's league. He'd taken the better part of his savings and invested in a ranch in Texas. He could never afford a place like this, too.

Addison Lombardo was a fool. He'd made a serious mistake using Jenna and Becca to draw Buck into this sick game. If, after all this time, he'd wanted to get back at Buck, he should have been man enough to face him without all the smoke and mirrors.

The gates opened, the Hummer rolled through and didn't stop until they reached the grand steps leading to the home's towering front entry. A wheelchair ramp ran parallel to the steps.

Definitely Addison Lombardo.

The two men got out of the vehicle and Buck did the same since no one told him otherwise.

"Are you carrying, Mr. Buchanan?" the thug who'd been driving asked as he approached Buck with a caution that spoke of professional training.

"I'd be a fool not to be."

The second thug came up behind Buck and patted him down. He discovered and took possession of the 9 mm Ruger pistol.

"This way, Mr. Buchanan."

Buck was escorted up the steps. The ornate double doors were opened and he crossed the threshold alone. His heart rate accelerated in anticipation of seeing Jenna and Becca released and getting this insanity over with.

"He's waiting in the library," the thug informed him. "Second door on your left." Then he closed the doors, leaving Buck alone in the entryhall.

Buck supposed the two would stand guard outside.

He kept his smile to himself. It wouldn't be long until they had company.

Now, to give Lombardo what he wanted. A face-off.

Doors on either side of the wide entry foyer led to massive parlors, a sweeping staircase showcased by a dazzling chandelier lay on the right directly ahead. Beyond that were more doors, as well as an elevator.

Buck headed for the second one on the left as instructed. If Lombardo wanted him dead, he needed to consider that, armed or not, Buck wasn't going down without a fight.

But first, he had to make sure the bastard lived up to his word that Jenna and Becca would be released. Considering the man's word had never been as good as it should have been, Buck hadn't taken any chances.

The note on the napkin had instructed his sister to contact George and Sheriff Sykes, followed by: Dark. Tonight. Buchanan Building. Everything at risk.

His sister wouldn't fail him.

Squaring his shoulders and bracing for battle, Buck entered the library. Aptly named, the room was lined with book-filled shelves.

There he was. Lombardo sat behind a broad polished desk, a pistol in his right hand.

"Welcome, Buck." His lips twisted into a smile. "Join me for a bit of catching up, won't you?" He gestured, while still holding the gun, to one of the chairs flanking his desk. "It's been a very long time."

Buck looked into the face of the man who had betrayed his own team, who had betrayed NASCAR. Buck realized that bitterness had eaten away anything at all good that had once been a part of this human being.

"Where are Jenna and Becca?" Buck demanded.

"The deal was, you got what you wanted and they would be released."

Lombardo waved him off dismissively. "Not to worry, Buck. I've already sent them on their way."

His words didn't ease Buck's mounting tension. It was more the words he used than the way he made the statement. Buck hoped his plan would work. The only way to be sure help arrived on time was to make sure Lombardo didn't make his final move too quickly.

"Why wait this long for me?" Buck asked as he took a seat. Logical question. One he was sure Lombardo would revel in explaining the answer to. If his intent had been to harm someone Buck cared about, why now? Why not last year or the year before that?

Lombardo chuckled, the sound harsh and laden with bitterness. "I didn't have time to deal with you in the beginning, Buchanan."

The tension in the air shifted abruptly. Buck felt the change as surely as he'd heard the man address him in a more formal manner. The old man's expression turned as somber as the grave.

"My wife was very ill," he explained. "Cancer. The tailspin you threw my professional life into finished her off. She just gave up. But the worst part was the disappointment in her eyes every time she looked at me until they closed for the last time." Lombardo nodded once. "You did that. *You* took everything I cared about away from me. Left me with nothing at all."

"I didn't know Martha had passed. I'm truly sorry

to hear about that," Buck said, his words genuine. Then he looked Lombardo straight in the eye and refrained from saying the rest of what he really wanted to. "You're right. *I* did that to you. Why not get straight to the point? There was no need to bring anyone else into it."

Lombardo's lips lifted into a knowing smile. "It took me years to figure out exactly how I was going to do this. I waited and waited for just the right moment. I had begun to think it wasn't coming, that you'd never get romantically involved again. You see, I needed to hurt you the way you'd hurt me." He thumped his chest. "Straight through the heart. And then your old friend McElroy gave me exactly what I needed."

Fury lit in Buck so fast it was all he could do to remain seated. He struggled to keep his true thoughts hidden. "Is that right? McElroy's been working with you, has he?"

Lombardo shook his head. "Don't give him that much credit, Buchanan. He still looks up to you a little, but jealousy caused him to behave badly.

"McElroy liked the status quo," Lombardo went on. "Whenever he felt that he was threatened he did something about it. Like when he urged you not to go after the woman you loved. McElroy believed Jenna didn't belong in your world, so he made sure to see that no one trusted her." Lombardo laughed outright. "When he told me what he'd done, it was almost worth the wait."

Buck restrained the need to lash out. He had to keep the old bastard talking until his backup arrived. "Things ended between Jenna and me because I was a fool," Buck suggested. "Maybe you're the one giving McElroy too much credit."

Lombardo shook his head. "No. You're just a bigger fool than you know, that's all. Your good friend kept the members of your own team pitted against her with his little comments and innuendoes of how she was turning you against them because she wanted you all to herself. All the while he distracted you from paying proper attention to her every chance he got. Until she'd had enough."

Why the hell would he have done that? Buck couldn't see what McElroy had hoped to gain.

"Once she was out of the way," Lombardo continued, "things went back to the way they used to be and your friend was happy again for a few more years. At least until your new driver started to get too close."

How could someone Buck had trusted so much have been so warped? Why hadn't he seen that side of Tom?

"Don't beat yourself up, Buchanan," Lombardo offered. "You never were *that* brilliant."

Enough. "Maybe not," Buck returned, "but I was smart enough to take you down."

Fury contorted the old man's face for a few seconds before he regained control. "Yes, you did. But I had the last laugh. McElroy was so angry when you turned on him that he decided to make you sorry. He came to me and told me about the child."

The fire of retaliation roaring in Buck's gut extinguished. "That's impossible. I didn't even know about her."

Amusement twinkled in those devilish eyes. "Ah, but your dear friend McElroy did. You see he kept an eye on Jenna for a while all those years ago just to make sure she didn't get any ideas about showing back up on your doorstep. Imagine his surprise when he learned she was expecting your child."

The idea that Tom McElroy had known for all those years and kept that knowledge from Buck sent a new wave of outrage blasting through him. If he survived this night, McElroy would be hearing from him.

"But then," Lombardo said, "when you kicked him off your team he decided to do something with that information. Something that would make you regret the day you were born. That's when he came to me and spilled his guts. Your closest confidant knew that you had never stopped pining for Jenna Williams. He knew you would love the child, no matter how you felt about offspring. He knew you too well, Buchanan. That was your big mistake."

The SOB would pay.

Buck would see to it.

"Do you have any idea how much pleasure your suffering has given me already?"

"I've given you what you wanted," Buck said,

wrestling with the fury that threatened to send him across that desk to strangle the old man, gun or no gun. "I need some kind of proof that you've released Jenna and Becca before we finish this business."

"That's the one thing about you, Buchanan," Lombardo said with a heavy exhale, "that I knew I could count on. I knew you'd do the right thing. You always do. It's enough to make a man sick," he snarled. "You always played by the rules, always the good guy, the damned hero. And still you managed to stay at the top."

His despisement for Buck hardened in his eyes. "But this time it won't do you any good. Nothing is going to change the way this ends."

Gunfire outside signaled to Buck that help had arrived. Thank God. "You won't win," he warned Lombardo. "Give up now and save yourself any more trouble." He glanced pointedly at the weapon in the old man's hand.

Lombardo laughed even as the commotion entered the house. The sound of running footsteps echoed in the massive hall right outside the room and he didn't so much as flinch.

"It's too late, old friend," Lombardo said. "I've already won. Now you will know how it feels to lose *everything*."

Lombardo raised the pistol toward his head. "I can die a happy man. And you, my friend, will live a long time—alone and miserable. Just like you deserve."

Without thinking, Buck bolted across the desk and reached for the gun. The momentum knocked both men to the floor as they wrestled for possession of the weapon.

The single gunshot echoed throughout the room.

"GET OUT."

Her heart thumping wildly, Jenna stared at the man dressed all in black and wearing a ski mask who had opened the rear doors of the cargo van. "Where are we?"

"Just get out!"

Becca pressed closer to her mother. "Mom?"

Jenna smiled, the effort shaky at best, in an attempt to reassure her. "It's okay, sweetie. Let's just do what the man says."

Jenna moistened her lips and prayed hard as she climbed out of the cargo area of the van, her hand wrapped tightly around her daughter's. Once she was out of the vehicle and looked around, even in the dark, she recognized where she was.

Buck's shop. This was where Buck and his team kept the car. As she recalled security was very tight here. A fence surrounded the perimeter of the property and there had always been armed guards.

"This way," the goon ordered. He indicated with the weapon he held that Jenna should go ahead of him.

Pulling her daughter close to her, Jenna walked toward the shop. As they neared the building a side door opened and another man dressed similarly to the first stepped out and said, "Everything's ready."

Renewed fear roared viciously through Jenna. She had no weapon. There was nothing she could do but follow orders and keep praying that help would come.

But how?

No one knew where they were.

"Please." Before Jenna could stop herself, she turned to face the man who had driven them here. "Let my daughter go. Please," she begged.

"Get inside."

He shoved Jenna forward. Becca cried out.

"It's okay," Jenna tried to console her daughter. She kept her arms tightly around her as the man forced them into the building.

Inside still looked much the same as she remembered. Shelving lined with products and large tool boxes wrapped the walls, interrupted only by the well-placed workbenches. In the center of it all stood No. 86. Her heart stumbled as she considered just how much this all meant to Buck. She'd spent years resenting all that racing meant to him. For what purpose? To end up keeping his daughter from him and believing she was right to do it.

She had been so wrong.

And now her daughter was paying the price for her past immaturity and her recent shortsightedness.

The second man tied their hands, intricately tethering each of them to one of the workbenches. The first man, the one who'd driven them here, approached and announced, "Time to go."

The two men walked out, thankfully without turning the lights off.

Jenna wiggled her hands, tried to stretch the nylon rope binding her. If she could get loose, she could untie Becca and they could get out of here and make a run for it as soon as the coast was clear. She still felt a little woozy, but she could do it.

"Mom, what's that smell?"

"What, honey?" Jenna stilled, sniffed the air.

At the same time that her daughter said, "That," Jenna smelled the odor. Not exactly strong but just pungent enough to make her grimace as her olfactory assimilated the scent.

It smelled like…lighter fluid.

Yes, lighter fluid. She'd had an uncle who smoked and he'd never used the disposable lighters, claimed they were useless. She remembered the silver Zippo lighter…and the fluid he'd used to fill it.

Oh, God!

Then she smelled the smoke.

Jenna twisted around to see where it was coming from. Her pulse rate jumped into panic mode.

She didn't see anything.

Where was it coming from?

Then she saw it. Seeping in beneath the door they'd entered.

She started to stretch at her bindings again. "Hurry, baby," she urged, "try to work your hands loose."

Her legs shook with terror. There was no way they would be able to get free if they didn't hurry.

A scraping sound abruptly shattered the silence.

Jenna's gaze shot toward the overhead garage door as it began its slow move upward.

Were those men going to shoot them now?

Jenna tugged at the ropes. Pulled as hard as she could.

"Jenna?"

Her attention snapped forward.

Lori?

Suddenly Lori Houser and Charlene Talley were rushing toward them. A cloud of smoke followed them inside the shop.

"Those men!" Jenna shouted. "Two of them! They're out there somewhere. They have guns."

"Don't worry," Lori said as she hurried toward her, "they left."

As Lori attempted to get Jenna loose, Charlene worked on the rope restraining Becca.

A loud pop sent Jenna's heart surging into her throat. "What was that?"

Lori shook her head. "I don't know but we've gotta get out of here." She glanced around. "We need something to cut this rope."

Jenna continued to fight the bindings, her heart slamming mercilessly against her sternum, as Lori moved from workbench to workbench searching for a cutting tool.

"This'll do." She returned with a hacksaw. Her gaze collided with Jenna's. "Don't move."

"No," Jenna argued. "Cut Becca loose first."

Lori nodded her understanding. Then, as Charlene held Becca's hands immobile, Lori cautiously cut through the ropes.

Once Becca was free, Lori said, "Get her out of here. Make sure the fire department is on the way."

Jenna's chest constricted as she watched Charlene flee the building with her daughter in tow. Becca kept looking back at her mother. Jenna kept a shaky smile in place for her.

"Go on, sweetie," she urged. "I'll be right behind you."

"Be still," Lori ordered.

No sooner than Charlene and Becca had escaped, another small explosion rent the air. This time both Lori and Jenna ducked for cover. The air had started to burn Jenna's lungs.

"It's the cleaning fluid," Lori explained as she rushed to saw at Jenna's ropes again. "We have to hurry! Why don't the sprinklers come on?" she snapped as she worked harder to free Jenna. "They should have come on already."

Jenna couldn't answer that question. She only knew that if they didn't hurry it would be too late to get out. The saw slipped, bit into Jenna's flesh. She cried out.

"Sorry," Lori muttered, but she didn't stop cutting.

The rope finally fell loose. Lori dropped the saw, grabbed Jenna by the arm and started to run.

Once they emerged from the building amid the billowing smoke, Jenna's movements slowed as she looked back. "What about Number eighty-six?" Her gaze bumped into Lori's. The flames around the exterior of the building were raging.

Lori tugged at her to get her moving again. "Come on. As long as you and Becca are safe that's all that matters."

Startled by her response, Jenna stumbled after her. Her legs felt heavy and out of sync with the rest of her body. The after effects of the drug she'd been given, she surmised.

At the edge of the woods across the road from the devastation, they all hovered and watched the flames build higher.

Jenna held her daughter close, the tears of gratitude flowing down her cheeks. "Thank you," she said to the women who had saved their lives. "How did you know?"

Lori shook her head. "We didn't. When Buck got the call from the kidnapper that he had to trade himself for the two of you, he sent a message to us through Reba that everything was at risk. The rest of the team, along with Sheriff Sykes and his men, got into position at the Buchanan Building since that's where Buck was told to go. George sent me and

Charlene here to keep an eye on things just in case
the everything meant *everything*. We'd no sooner
parked over here—" she nodded to the side road next
to where they stood "—than the van arrived with you
guys. If we'd gotten here just a few seconds later,
those thugs would have spotted us and we'd all be
tied up in there." Her gaze shifted back to the shop
where the fire was slowly but surely engulfing the
building.

The first thing she'd said was still churning around
in Jenna's head. Somewhere in the distance the sound
of sirens screamed.

"What do you mean Buck traded himself for us?"

Lori shrugged.

Something else inside the shop exploded.

"Damn!" Charlene shouted. "The whole place is
going to burn down before help gets here."

"Tell me," Jenna urged Lori. "Where's Buck?"

Lori's eyes locked with hers. "I don't know."

The sound of roaring engines and flashing lights
drew their attention to the road. Three county police
cruisers came to rocking halts on the road between
where they stood and the burning shop. Two of the
deputies rushed over. "You ladies all right?"

Jenna nodded, the realization that her daughter was
safe sending a new surge of tears down her cheeks.

But what about Buck? Please let him be safe, too.

Two ambulances and three fire trucks arrived and
then there was official personnel everywhere. While

a paramedic checked Becca out, Jenna kept asking anyone who passed about Buck.

Why couldn't somebody tell her something?

"Jenna."

She whipped around at the sound of his voice. Her heart jumped wildly in her chest.

It was him.

She rushed into Buck's arms. "I was so worried."

He hugged her long and hard. "I'm fine." He drew back then and surveyed her top to bottom and back. "He didn't hurt you?"

She shook her head. "We're okay."

Buck glanced past her and his breath caught. Even if she hadn't heard the sharp sound she would have seen the fascination claim his expression.

She tugged him over to where the paramedic had just finished his exam of Becca. "Could you excuse us a moment?"

"Sure thing." The man stepped around to the front of his ambulance.

Jenna smiled at her daughter. "Becca," she said, her voice trembling just a little, "this is Buck Buchanan."

Becca looked at Buck, then at her mom, the question in her eyes.

Jenna nodded in answer. "This is your father."

Buck stuck out his hand. "Hello, Becca."

Becca studied his hand a moment, then she cautiously placed hers in his wide palm. "It's very nice to meet you."

Buck laughed and so did Jenna. And then they all hugged.

Whatever would happen after this night, Jenna couldn't be sure about, but they were safe. And that was all that really mattered.

CHAPTER FIFTEEN

Race Day
Daytona Beach, Florida

JENNA PARKED her rented car amid the sea of others. She and Becca had flown into Daytona Beach early that morning. Evidently not early enough, she decided, judging by the sheer number of fans already on site.

"Are all these people here for the race?"

She smiled at Becca. "Yep. NASCAR has lots of fans. This is one of the biggest races of the season." The excitement was undeniable. As much as she'd once dreaded these moments since she knew that they would only take Buck away from her, she couldn't pretend the energy wasn't real. Even she had felt it. The sensation was more powerful now.

Becca peered out across the parking lot. "You think we'll be able to find him in this crowd?"

Jenna's smile widened to a grin. "Yep."

She and her daughter made their way to the security station. "Jenna Williams," she told the guard as she presented her driver's license as ID. "And Becca Williams."

"Go right on in, Ms. Williams." The guard smiled at Becca as he handed them their passes. "Mr. Buchanan is expecting you."

Both put the passes around their necks before Jenna held Becca's hand as they made their way to the hauler emblazoned with the Rocket City Racers logo. She knew that was where Buck would be— with No. 86 and his driver. With the fans.

Luckily the sprinkler system at the shop had kicked in and slowed the interior fire enough to save the car. But even that wouldn't have been enough had the fire department not arrived in such a timely manner. Lombardo's henchmen had tampered with the building's security system but the built-in secondary system had proven worth its weight in gold. The sprinklers had been engaged and the fire department notified even before Charlene Talley had made her call. Thankfully, the two security guards had still been alive. The two men had been bound and gagged and then locked in one of the storerooms inside the shop.

As Jenna neared the group, familiar faces stood out. The team. Fans. Everyone wanted to touch stardom…to feel the power of a winner.

This was part of what Jenna had struggled with before. But she'd been wrong. Buck's dedication to the sport and to his team didn't mean that he didn't love her enough. He'd proved that the instant he agreed to help her, not to mention willingly trading himself for her and her child. She would never forget that act of heroism, of selflessness.

Buck had explained everything to her. The members of his team had been turned against her all those years ago by one of their own. Even so, Lori and Charlene had willingly risked their lives to save her and Becca.

Jenna owed them a large debt of gratitude as well as a definite second chance at being friends.

Though she hadn't been able to come down to Daytona with Buck earlier in the week because of school and work, Jenna and Becca had been invited all the same. That she and Becca were here now was the first step in many more to come.

And Buck, she thought as her gaze collided with his, he was simply Buck. Charming and handsome, and the man with whom she wanted to renew the love that still burned deep inside her.

And no matter how much he loved those people surrounding him right now she knew—finally *knew*—he cared more for her. And for Becca. Maybe she'd been too young all those years ago. She wasn't that naive, frightened little girl anymore. She was a woman and *he* was her man.

Addison Lombardo had almost taken this chance from them. One of his thugs had posed as a technician from Buck's security company. He'd planted monitors, audio and visual, in Buck's home. Similar bugs had been placed in Buck's cell phone, in the shop and at his office, as well as at Jenna's home and in her cell phone. He'd covered every single base but one—plain old ingenuity. There was no way to stop a man like Buck Buchanan and the people who trusted and respected him.

Buck excused himself and walked over to meet Jenna and Becca.

He offered his hand to his daughter to shake in greeting. She giggled and shook hands. They were taking small steps but Becca liked him a lot. Jenna had known she would fall quickly. Everyone fell hard and fast for Buck Buchanan.

Buck hugged Jenna. "I'm glad you're here," he whispered in her ear. Then he drew back far enough to look into her eyes. "Thanks."

"You show your daughter how a race is won and I'll be happy," she teased.

Buck squeezed her hand and then he had to go back to the business of being Buck Buchanan, racing legend.

Becca was already off with George having a last look at No. 86 before the race.

"He's happier than I've seen him in a long time." Jenna turned to face Lori Houser. "He is. And so am I." It was true. Jenna loved that her daughter had her father in her life. She only wished that she and Buck had worked things out sooner. Then again, all things happened for a reason and in their own time. Their time had come now. "And my daughter is ecstatic."

"She's beautiful, Jenna." Lori smiled. "Later, I'll introduce you to my kids. I have a daughter just a year younger than Becca. Her name is Emily. I'm sure they'll be fast friends."

Jenna returned the smile. "Thanks. I'm certain you're right." She watched Becca accepting a hug from Rush. Her daughter thought Rush was hot. Every day there was something new with her swiftly growing up pre-teen. She was going to be ready for Juilliard way before Jenna could catch her breath.

"There's Charlie from the *Florida Tribune*." Lori waved at the man in question. "I'll catch you later, Jenna."

Jenna watched her merge into the fray to do what she did best, captivating the members of media.

Not an easy task, especially with a man like Lombardo orchestrating trouble. But he was getting what he deserved now. Buck had told her what had happened. As they wrestled with the gun, Lombardo tried to kill himself but, thanks to Buck, had missed. The bullet hit the wall behind him instead.

Thank God Buck wasn't hurt.

Lombardo had been charged with numerous felonies, including kidnapping, and was being held without bail. His cohorts were being rounded up, including Tom McElroy, who had been charged with conspiracy to commit felony kidnapping for his part in what happened.

Life was back to normal now, at least as normal as life with a new NASCAR season heating up allowed.

"We need to have a little talk, Ms. Williams."

Jenna snapped out of her thoughts to find Buck standing right next to her. He took her hand and lured her off to the trailer where the driver and the team took breaks from the insanity.

"What?" It was almost race time. She was surprised that he dared divert his attention even for a moment.

Once inside he backed her against the closed door. "I know we're supposed to be taking this slow, one step at a time."

"Baby steps," she reminded. "And there's a lot of ground to cover before—"

"Before we make any major decisions," he finished for her. "I know." He brushed a kiss across her lips. "We're taking our time. No hurry." Another of those feathery kisses stroked her mouth. "But right now we have maybe five minutes. Do you think…?"

She grinned and pushed her arms up and around his neck. "Definitely."

He kissed her and the rest of the world faded away. It was just the two of them…sharing one of many, many special moments to come.

They had a rare second chance at making this right. She, for one, intended to do her part.

* * * * *

Happily ever after is just the beginning...

Turn the page for a sneak preview of
A HEARTBEAT AWAY
by
Eleanor Jones

Harlequin Everlasting—Every great love
has a story to tell. ™
A brand-new series from Harlequin Books

Special? A prickle ran down my neck and my heart started to beat in my ears. Was today really special?

"Tuck in," he ordered.

I turned my attention to the feast that he had spread out on the ground. Thick, home-cooked-ham sandwiches, sausage rolls fresh from the oven and a huge variety of mouthwatering scones and pastries. Hunger pangs took over, and I closed my eyes and bit into soft homemade bread.

When we were finally finished, I lay back against the bluebells with a groan, clutching my stomach.

Daniel laughed. "Your eyes are bigger than your stomach," he told me.

I leaned across to deliver a punch to his arm, but he rolled away, and when my fist met fresh air I collapsed in a fit of giggles before relaxing on my back and staring up into the flawless blue sky. We lay like that for quite a while, Daniel and I, side by side in companionable silence, until he stretched out his hand in an arc that encompassed the whole area.

"Don't you think that this is the most beautiful place in the entire world?"

His voice held a passion that echoed my own feelings, and I rose onto my elbow and picked a buttercup to hide the emotion that clogged my throat.

"Roll over onto your back," I urged, prodding him with my forefinger. He obliged with a broad grin, and I reached across to place the yellow flower beneath his chin.

"Now, let us see if you like butter."

When a yellow light shone on the tanned skin below his jaw, I laughed.

"There…you do."

For an instant our eyes met, and I had the strangest sense that I was drowning in those honey-brown depths. The scent of bluebells engulfed me. A roaring filled my ears, and then, unexpectedly, in one smooth movement Daniel rolled me onto my back and plucked a buttercup of his own.

"And do *you* like butter, Lucy McTavish?" he asked. When he placed the flower against my skin, time stood still.

His long lean body was suspended over mine, pinning me against the grass. Daniel…dear, comfortable, familiar Daniel was suddenly bringing out in me the strangest sensations.

"Do you, Lucy McTavish?" he asked again, his voice low and vibrant.

My eyes flickered toward his, the whisper of a sigh escaped my lips and although a strange lethargy had crept into my limbs, I somehow felt as if all my nerve endings were on fire. He felt it, too—I could see it in his warm brown eyes. And when he lowered his face to mine, it seemed to me the most natural thing in the world.

None of the kisses I had ever experienced could have even begun to prepare me for the feel of Daniel's lips on mine. My entire body floated on a tide of ecstasy that shut out everything but his soft, warm mouth, and I knew that this was what I had been waiting for the whole of my life.

"Oh, Lucy." He pulled away to look into my eyes. "Why haven't we done this before?"

Holding his gaze, I gently touched his cheek, then I curled my fingers through the short thick hair at the base of his skull, overwhelmed by the longing to drown again in the sensations that flooded our bodies. And when his long tanned fingers crept across my tingling skin, I knew I could deny him nothing.

* * * * *

*Be sure to look for
A HEARTBEAT AWAY,
available February 27, 2007.*

*And look, too, for
THE DEPTH OF LOVE
by Margot Early,
the story of a couple who must learn
that love comes in many guises—and in the end
it's the only thing that counts.*

**Hearts racing
Blood pumping
Pulses accelerating**

Falling in love can be
a blur...especially at
180 mph!

So if you crave the thrill
of the chase—on and off
the track—you'll love

SPEED BUMPS
by Ken Casper!

On sale May 2007

www.GetYourHeartRacing.com

Hearts racing
Blood pumping
Pulses accelerating

Falling in love can be
a blur...especially at
180 mph!

So if you crave the thrill
of the chase—on and off
the track—you'll love

SPEED BUMPS
by Ken Casper!

On sale May 2007

www.GetYourHeartRacing.com

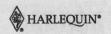

REQUEST YOUR FREE BOOKS!
2 FREE NOVELS PLUS 2 FREE GIFTS!

TM *Silhouette*®

S P E C I A L   E D I T I O N®

Life, Love and Family!

SSE07